The Streets Will Never Close 3

Lock Down Publications and
Ca$h
Presents
The Streets Will Never Close 3
A Novel by *K'ajji*

Lock Down Publications
P.O. Box 944
Stockbridge, Ga 30281
www.lockdownpublications.com

Copyright 2022 K'ajji
The Streets Will Never Close 3

All rights reserved. No part of this book may be reproduced in any form or by electronic or mechanical means, including information storage and retrieval systems without permission in writing from the publisher, except by a reviewer who may quote brief passages in review.

First Edition March 2022
Printed in the United States of America

This is a work of fiction. Names, characters, places, and incidents either are products of the author's imagination or are used fictitiously. Any similarity to actual events or locales or persons, living or dead, is entirely coincidental.

Lock Down Publications
Like our page on Facebook: Lock Down Publications @
www.facebook.com/lockdownpublications.ldp
Book interior design by: **Shawn Walker**
Edited by: **Cassandra Sims**

K'ajji

Stay Connected with Us!

Text **LOCKDOWN** to 22828 to stay up-to-date with new releases, sneak peaks, contests and more...

Thank you!

Submission Guideline.

Submit the first three chapters of your completed manuscript to ldpsubmissions@gmail.com, subject line: Your book's title. The manuscript must be in a .doc file and sent as an attachment. Document should be in Times New Roman, double spaced and in size 12 font. Also, provide your synopsis and full contact information. If sending multiple submissions, they must each be in a separate email.

Have a story but no way to send it electronically? You can still submit to LDP/Ca$h Presents. Send in the first three chapters, written or typed, of your completed manuscript to:

LDP: Submissions Dept
P.O. Box 944
Stockbridge, Ga 30281

DO NOT send original manuscript. Must be a duplicate.

Provide your synopsis and a cover letter containing your full contact information.

Thanks for considering LDP and Ca$h Presents.

K'ajji

CHAPTER 1
GORILLA WARFARE
Six

Day 74....

It was 7:33 am. He should've been on his way out to take his daughter to school any minute now. We'd seen him on his route quite a few—hold up, aw shit! The door just opened. I slowly creeped from under the house, hoping I was undetected. I ain't wanna do it like this. Shorty gon' hate apes forever after witnessin' this shit. But it is what it is. I pulled the hammer back on the Smith & Wesson in a crouching position on the side of the house.

"I'll be right back, Meik! Damn!" I heard his voice, the screen door opened, then a loud thud. I could hear the thumps as they'd walked down the wooden steps of the porch. "Come on, Chelle, we late," he told his little one.

Comin' from one side of the house with my gun raised, I was behind him as he held her hand. He'd heard movement and turned to look at me. I let go. It only took the one slug I sent through his face, opening up the back of his head. His daughter hadn't noticed me until she heard the thundering blast of the cannon, and her father was ripped from her fingertips by the impact of the slug. I'll never forget her eyes. Her screams, or how she was lookin' up at me at this very moment. A lil bit of blood was splattered across her face, her French braids and her Rainbow Bright backpack—her father's blood.

Takin' off runnin' across the street, it felt like I was moving in slow motion. There was no snow on the ground, but the freezing still air was making it so I witnessed every breath I exhaled through the mask. As my feet stomped across the asphalt of a newly paved driveway, I almost lost my footing and fell. It was still kinda dark out. It was a good thing Telesis right in front of me moving as my guide toward our getaway plan. I was breathin' harder than a muthafucka! I could hear pounding in my chest. My adrenalin. My mind racing, I was subjected to my every thought surrounding me. Clothesline, duck! Run! Fence—jump! Okay, cross the alley! We're across the alley. Next yard. Fence, jump, nigga! Cleared that bitch. Side of the house! Almost there. *Go! Go! Go-go!*

I was halfway in, and the door wasn't even shut all the way. I'm at Smoke. "Go, my nigga!"

He pulled off, he said, "Y'all get'em?"

As Telesis laid on the floor, I dove across the back seat of the stolen Buick.

"Yeah! I-I got his ho-ass." I was outta breath, but good.

Telesis laughed and said, "Damn! Smoke, you should've seen it! That nigga's head exploded like a fuckin' pumpkin'! Ha—haaa!" She'd tried to raise up, but I pushed her ass back down.

"Lesis, stop playin' girl! Stay the fuck down!" I yelled.

We'd made it off the North side without incident. Since we were already at the lake disposing of the weapon, I had Smoke drop me off at Honesty's. She was up waitin' on me too. She had a million questions about why she couldn't get in contact with me, after I'd told her I was comin' over. I was drained, tired and hungry. I wasn't in the mood to argue. I'd told her my battery was dead, but she wasn't having that. She swore up and down I was cheatin' on her. After snatchin' my pager, she stormed off into the bedroom and slammed the door. I wasn't trippin' on that. Wasn't shit in there for her to see. I'd erased all the pages she'd sent me, along with everybody else. I walked in the bedroom behind her. I had to get out of this gear.

"Why yo' pants and shit all dirty?" she asked me, with her nose all curled to the side.

"We got to squabbin' with some niggaz last night at the bar. I thought you was mad? You find what you was lookin' for?" I asked, comin' outta my coat, shoes, then my shirt. She had a fit!

"Uh-unnnnn! Take yo' ass in the bathroom wit' all that shit! You—is-not-at—home!" she yelled.

Gettin' off the bed, she pushed me towards the door.

"Honesty, come on now! I gotta get some clean clothes and shit." I reached for the closet, but she pushed my hand down.

"Don't! Don't touch nothin'! Just gone in the bathroom! I'll get everything else. Gone! I ain't playin' witchu Marcus! Come on.

The Streets Will Never Close 3

You smell like outside." She grabbed me by my hand and led me to the bathroom, while holding my shirt between two of her fingers as if it was contaminated.

When we got in the bathroom, she threw my shit in the dirty clothes hamper and turned on the shower.

She said, "Getcho ass in there. I'll be back. Throw the rest of that shit in the hamper, too."

As I was gettin' undressed, I saw her come out of the room carryin' my Nikes like they too had a disease.

"Hold up, babe! Where you goin' with my shoes?"

"On the balcony!" she yelled over her shoulder. Them mufuckas dirty as shit. I might as well throw 'em away."

When the shower hit me, it felt so relaxing and soothing at first, but then his daughter's face flashed in my mind. I could hear her screams echoing inside.

"Damn, shorty. He had to go." I musta unconsciously said what I was thinkin' out loud.

Unknowingly, Honesty was right there next to the shower when I opened my eyes.

She said, "Whatchu say? I know you ain't trippin' 'bout them damn shoes? It's some blood on 'em, too. I guess you wasn't lyin' about gettin' into it. Slide to the front some, let me in." She disrobed. I adjusted the water temperature, and she got in behind me. "Here, gimme your towel," she whispered seductively in my ear.

I handed it to her, and she lathered it up to wash my back.

I turned and said, "Honesty, don't mess wit' my ass now!"

She laughed, "Boi, I ain't gon' go up in yo' butt crack! Turn around! Shit! That's yo' job, buddy."

I gave her my back. "I know! And you laughin'. Don't act like you ain't tried to before."

She began to wash me up. "Aw, stop cryin'. I'm gon' wash everything else, including these little cheeks you got back here. Is that a problem?" she asked.

"Nah, just don't go nowhere near my shitter."

After she washed my body, I hit the spots she hadn't. I then took her towel and began to gently wash her back. When I got to the scar

9

on her chest, I caressed her damaged tissue with the towel, and traced it with my fingertips. My hands started shakin' as I did, I had no remorse in the fact I'd murdered Mighty, but the guilt of being responsible for her wound still got to me. It really bothered me. She musta felt I'd stayed in that area too long, because she opened her eyes and grabbed my hands. I was still shaking.

"Marcus, what's wrong? Why you shakin' like this?" She covered her scar. Her eyes veered from mine to the shower floor. "It's my scar, huh? You think my body ugly now don't chu?"

"Naw, baby. Look at me." I raised her chin. "You're beautiful. I love you. Every inch of you." She was still tense. I said, "Relax. Close your eyes and let me finish." She was reluctant, but she did as I'd asked, letting her guard down. "Put cha head back. Let me get cha neck, bae." I ran the cloth across her neck, breasts, shoulders and her stomach. I told her, "I just feel like—like I did this to you. Me bein' who I am caused you this pain. It's my fault, and I'm sorry baby."

She looked me straight in my eyes and said, "I don't blame you, so don't start blaming yourself. Them niggaz ain't give a damn who the fuck they was shootin' at when they came through the hood and did this to us. Don't let 'em win, a'ight! Cause I'm sure you ain't know no shit like dat was gon' happen, or you wouldn't have been there. You've never brought drama to your home front. Never will I let you take the blame for what them bitch ass niggaz did to me! You understand?"

"I love you so much," I told her as I rinsed her body, then kissed the scar on her chest. "Don't chu ever doubt that. Okay?" I whispered in her ear.

One thing led to another, and we ended up in the bedroom making love like never before. My bae is an old soul and loves digging in her mother's stash. We made love to song after song. *Secret Garden! Don't Disturb This Groove! Marvin Gaye's Sexual Healing* and more. I was no longer drained or hungry, as I licked and sucked her body. I was fully energized, as I stroked her love cave. Love is powerful like that. We went at it for hours. I spent the next few days at her house.

The Streets Will Never Close 3

No hustlin', just chillin' with my baby. We had movie nights. When we ran out of those, we watched a bunch of old episodes of 227 and the Cosby Show she'd recorded onto VHS tapes. The characters Lester, Shondra and Brenda grew on me fast. Oh, and the old lady Pearl that stayed in the window tryna be nosey. Regina King was Honesty's favorite actor. I liked Jackee's portrayal as Shondra, the horny lady from upstairs. Them titties was huge! I wasn't really up on the show. I'd always loved the Cosby Show though. Love me some Phylicia Rashad.

It's something about her eyes that seemed so genuine, seductive and strong. Everything about her said, Essence, Queen, Wife and Ruler of her domain. It was what I expected if we were ever to get married. Of course Vanessa and Denise, played by Lisa and Tempest were beautiful as well. Clair Huxtable was just different for me. She said, *WOMAN* in all capital letters.

Always grindin' and on the move, I never really had much time for TV, but I loved this message I was receiving. Next month, Honesty would be starting at U.W. Parkside to become a Dermatologist. She was well on her way to becoming the woman she wants to be, and I'm proud. Me, I'm knee deep in the game, sittin' here eatin' a big ass bowl of Captain Crunch, watchin' Cliff's depiction of a man, as I wonder if dreams really come true for street niggaz?

K'ajji

CHAPTER 2
LEGENDARY
Proof

On the Northside, the distinct smell of stale cigarettes, liquor and weed filled the atmosphere. At Tameiko's request, D.J. Tiny Tim had just finished spinning *Always* by *Atlantic Starr*, then changed it to *Secret Lovers*, taking Meiko back to her first days with her long lost love. Her now ex-best friend's Tamara's man. Being that they'd both bore his child, for years they'd fought for his affection. Now, neither of them had him. The formidable Mighty Mike was gone. All she had left now were pictures, memories, and their daughter Terchelle.

Peoples was packed with mourners wearing t-shirts bearing his name. Tears drenching her face, Tameiko danced alone holding a fifth of Gin she'd talked me into buying for her. I'm thinking, the funeral hadn't even took place yet, and if she was fucked up like this already! Damn. As me and Congo looked on from the corner of the bar, the guilt became more overwhelming for me then I could stand.

"I can't believe my nigga gone, Congo. Out of all the shit we've been through. All the fights and gun battles! Legendary, but my nigga gone. I ain't gon' never see 'em no more. I'm tired of this shit. I gotta holla at Zoo and Tee." I got up to head in their direction, but Congo grabbed my arm. "Hold up, Lawd. Whatchu about to go holla at them niggas about?" he asked.

"I know who kilt him," I replied, as a tear fell from my eye.

His eyes bucked. "You know who killed who?"

"I know who kilt them all. Wolfy, Lobo, Rise Mase, Jungle and Mighty." I sighed.

"Damn, Lawd! How you know?" Congo looked around nervously.

"Cause, Me and Mighty was buggin' one night. We went and done some dumb shit, knowing it was supposed to be peace. The lil' chicks that got shot up on the Eastside..." I dropped my head. "We did that. I know it gotta be them niggas. They figured out it was us somehow, I know it." Congo took a gulp of his Crown Royal.

"That was y'all, huh?" He shook his head. "I knew, I just ain't said shit. I'm just glad Stain wasn't with you niggas. I know how lil' bruh like to run with y'all crowd."

I said, "Yeah, luckily, Lewanna had his ass strung up. You can probably guess without me saying how I feel about vengeance, right?"

"It's mandatory," I said, using the words of young D. Stain.

"Exactly, but, you know what you about to tell them niggaz can easliy get you killed, right, Lawd?" Congo asked.

"Yeah, I know. But I don't got no other option. I can't war with them niggas by myself. I ain't shit without my homeboys. I'm dead without y'all."

He said, "I feel you. But just this morning Tee told me that knowing what's goin' on got him feeling out of touch with the streets. He's definitely ready to kill somethin'. It's a good chance Zoo might take y'all indignities to heart and murder you right here in front of everybody. I mean, who gon' say somethin'? He the king now. Ain't nobody got the balls to question his judgment. We ain't got no say. He's judge, jury and executioner around this bitch. And you know how J.L. got down."

I said, "Yeah, I know."

He said, "But if that's what you wanna do, Lawd, I'll walk over there with you."

I told him, "Shit, fuck it. Walk over here with me then." I threw my double shot of Vodka back, taking it to the head. Slammin' the empty glass on the table. "I'm good." I tried to convince myself.

Congo said, "Damn, nigga. You ready, huh? Hold on." He took a long guzzle of his Old English, and set the mug down. "Come on, Lawd."

CHAPTER 3
THE GOOD DIE YOUNG
Proof

I don't plan on dyin' tonight, or just lettin' no nigga demonstrate on me like they done niggas in the past. I know what Congo was sayin', and it's true. They could and probably would try to kill me, if they felt an example needed to be set in stone. I'd seen it happen to niggas, and it didn't matter who they were. Once a nigga's brains is on the table ain't no more thinkin' past that. Inside the right pocket of my Triple FAT Goose, my finger rested on the trigger of my Lugar.

As we approached Zoo and U-Tee, they had a lot of our niggas surrounding them. KRS-One's *Loves Gonna Getcha* shook the walls of the establishment. Everything seemed to be movin' in slow motion. When we got to the table, I had to actually yell over the song's 808 bass drum.

"Zoo, Tee! Let me holla at y'all real quick!" Tee's words to me seemed slurred and drawn out. Maybe I was just faded.

"Prooof? What up, laaawd!"

Here he go again, fuckin' wit' me, I thought.

"Y'all niggas excuse us for a second," he said, "let me holla at my oldest boy." As they stood up to greet me, I had to take my hand off of my gun to shake theirs.

Zoo said, "What up? Have a seat nigga." We all sat down.

"How ya momma doin'?" Tee asked.

"She doin'." I paused. "Look, I ain't gone bullshit you or my man sittin' right here. Im'a get straight to the point. I know who smoked cuz and nem, Mighty, and our other niggas."

"Hold up, Proof." Zoo looked me straight in my eyes as he placed his .45 on the table. "A'ight, go ahead."

"It was me and Mighty fault." I sighed. "We fucked up. One night, we went East and did a drive—" Tee put his hand up, cutting me off mid-sentence. Zoo looked at his gun, then the ceiling as he struggled to keep his composure.

I continued. "We fucked up!" Zoo snatched his gun off the table, but Tee grabbed him.

Zoo yelled, "You damn right y'all fucked up! I should kill yo' muthafukin' ass right now!"

Tee held on to Zoo's arm. "If it wasn't for yo' momma ... you, you know better," he said as he shook his head. "It can't happen Zoo! Let me handle this, a'ight!"

"A'ight. I'm good, my nigga," Zoo replied, but he never took his eyes off me.

"You good?" Tee double-checked.

"Yeah, let me go." All eyes were on us, as Zoo slowly sat his gun back down on the table.

As they sat back down, I pulled my gun from under the table and sat it next to his. All three of us had tears in our eyes.

See, U-Tee raised me. It's the only reason I had doubts on them killin' me. When we first moved up here from the *Chi*, him and my momma hit it off. I was only eight years old back then.

Though they were no longer together, they had been a couple for five years. To a lot of niggas in the hood, U-Tee was like a father or a big homie. But to me, he was a father. I've never met my real one, so U-Tee was the only pops I've ever known. And I had been disloyal. I'd betrayed their trust.

Zoo said, "Now, tell us what happened, Proof? Why did y'all disobey me?"

I really didn't have an answer for that. But I told'em how we'd went over there. How I'd tried to talk Mighty out of it after seeing all the females out there. I told'em about the ultimatum. How I decided to ride, rather than leave'em. It didn't mean shit. I was just takin' responsibility for my actions. Because even though I ain't dead, I know I'm far from being in the clear. I knew I had to be dealt wit'. By remaining silent about what happened, I'd caused too many of our people to lose their lives. I was out of order, period. Once I was done explaining, I would have to face the consequences.

CHAPTER 4
Exception

Zoo announced that we'd have a gathering the following day at three. He said, "Proof, you know what y'all find coulda' got me killed, right?"
I nodded my understanding.
Tee said, "It could've got us all fucked up! And to not say shit all this time. You make your way to see my sister before the sun come back up. We'll talk some more tomorrow." He and Zoo got up and walked off on me.
Tee being who he is, he's always been one to think ahead. He called up to Joliet, Illinois the next day and got his brother Big I to come down and handle the violation. He didn't want any of the niggas around us to put their hands on me. Some of them feared me, which made it likely that they wouldn't have handled the situation properly. Zoo felt the guys around us might lose respect for me if they had to carry out the discipline against me. I knew he just wanted my ass disciplined, fast and appropriately.
Ultimately, I was fined fifty racks, and had to accept a three-hunnid seconds beat down from head to toe, and I wasn't allowed to block any punches or kicks. They had Big I, and another nigga from home, put sticks on me. When it was over, I was fucked up! Those five minutes seemed to go on forever. I think my ribs were cracked, my eyes were swollen shut, and my lips were fucked too. *I could feel 'em balloonin'. I wasn't goin' to no hospital. I'ma soulja.*
Shit, I was still stretched out on the basement floor, bleedin'. I asked Zoo to give me a week before we took niggas to war. Although I'd fucked up, I wanted blood for my niggas. I knew that would be their next move.
Zoo warned me that if I ever disobeyed or disrespected him again, I'd best disappear, or he'd *make me* disappear. I knew he meant it, as painful as it was, Tee pulled me to my feet and hugged me. I put it on the fin that I'd never cross 'em again.
"You do know Im'a gangsta, right?" Tee laughed. "All is well between us, son. It's all good, you hear me?"

K'ajji

"Nigga, you're our G," said Zoo. "Y'all my muthafuckin' Vice Lords," I said. It hurt when I tried to laugh. My jaw felt broken.

CHAPTER 5
Honesty

I ain't say nothing to Marcus, but when I got up yesterday to make us same breakfast, I saw some shit on the news saying a dude name Michael Turaer was shot to death in front of his house early Friday morning. I remember one of the FBI dudes mentioning that name. While lying in the hospital, I also recall Six saying, "I know who shot y'all. I don't want you to worry. I'ma make them niggaz suffer." Then, I thought about the conversation in the car.
"Uh-un. We ain't never heard of the nigga, remember? He don't exist. At least he won't for long anyway."
When they flashed the picture of the dude, I could've sworn I'd seen him at the mall a few times. He would smile at me, like he knew me or some shit. Hell, I ain't tha sharpest knife in tha drawer, but I'm in there. The nigga came in here Friday morning with blood all on his shoes. It don't take a rocket scientist to put two and two together. That's why I went and got them shoes and everything he had on that morning, off the balcony. I got rid of it all. Coat, drawers, socks and everything. Im'a say somethin' to'em when I get off work. Ain't no tellin' what else he got layin' around. I don't want my baby downtown fighting no damn murder charges.
I ain't gon' ask him too many questions either. Matter of fact, I'm gon' put it to'em in *ifs*. I'll tell'em what I saw on the news, and simply tell'em *if* he had anything to do wit' it to get rid of everything that I hadn't. He gotta make sure he covers up all of his tracks. Maybe I'm trippin'; if so, he gon' be mad as hell about me throwing his leather coat in the dumpster. Oh well, better safe than sorry. Aw hell, here we go. I'm pulling in the parking lot at work now. Lord give me strength. You know Im'a need it. . . .
I pray I don't have to beat the brakes off one of these old white people, or one of these prissy bitches at the nurse's station. I don't know why they're always after me, but they get on my damn nerves. I'm here, though. Another day, another dollar. *It's just another day, Honesty. Stay focused,* I told myself as I climbed out of my little Honda and walked into the building.

As soon as I entered, I was greeted by Hatcher. This is one of the stankin' ass nurses that's always acting like she's better than somebody. She's been trying to get me fired for a year and a half. A bitch only been here two.

She said, "Why, hello Ms. Brown. Glad to see you've made it back."

"Em-hmm. Tuh, hey Hatch." *I hate a fake ass hoe!* I thought to myself. I wanna cuss her ass out for even speaking to me. But she was my shift supervisor, So, I walked past her, taking off my coat and scarf. I was on my way to the lounge when she called out to me. Fuckin' with me already.

"Honesty honey! You know the rules. The first thing you're supposed to do is look at the register chart to—"

"I know, Hatch. I'm gone see who my patients are for the day as soon as I hang up my coat!" I yelled without even looking in her direction. When I got to the lounge, I expected to see Ushi, Nichole, and a few more people, but I didn't. The place seemed so empty. I guess I'm just early. They'd be here soon.

Hanging up my coat, I'm on my way to see whose ass I'll be wipin' today before my shift starts. Looking at the chart, I'm happy to see Ms. Johnson's name. No Mrs. Goldstein today, but I'm gone make it my business to stop in and check on her anyway. I've got a few more bodies I'm not familiar with. I'll have to check the ladies and see what their history is like as soon as I see 'em. Right now, Im'a go see Ms. Jay. That's what I call Ms. Johnson. Walking the hallway, I'm seeing a few familiar faces. Residents, CNA's, and Nurses. Here I am at Ms. Jay's door. I peek in.

"Knock! Knock!" I yelled, tapping on the door before I entered, although it was open. She was lying in bed when she saw me and tried to force a smile. But the tears were still running down her face. "Heyyy Ms. Jay, I've missed youuu. What's wrong?" I asked.

"Hey, Honesty, baby. How have you been?" she replied.

"I'm doin' okay. How about yourself? Why are you up in here cryin'?"

"I just received some bad news from my family. That's all, baby." She wiped her face.

I grabbed her some Kleenex. "What kind of bad news? I know I'm being nosey. Please forgive me. I just wanna know what pains you."

"My grandson was killed the other day. I don't think you would've known him. He was in them streets. I know you don't be out there. You're a good girl."

"Ooooh! I'm sorry to hear that. I've probably heard of him. What's his name?"

"Mike. Emm-hm, Michael Turner. They say he was killed in front of my eight-year-old grandbaby. She's having trouble sleeping at night." I swear, I felt my heart skip a beat as I hugged her.

"I'm so sorry, Ms. Jay. No, I've never heard of, nor met, a Michael Turner."

K'ajji

CHAPTER 6
THE MATRIX
Crook

My big cousin, Triggs, brought in his twenty-first birthday in style at The Matrix. We out here off East Capitol, and this hoe jumpin'! Yeeeah, it's supposed to be twenty-one and over, but we in here. Fuck it! Flava Flav's voice was bangin' from the monitors, tellin' us to *Fight the Power*. When I saw something leaving the floor, I just had to follow. I tapped Brew to get his attention. We were both blitzed off the weed and the drank we had just before we walked up in this piece. We were on cloud nine.

"Damn! On the G, come on wit me real quick." I tugged at his sleeve.

He said, "Nigga, where the hell you goin'?" he wanted another drink. But I was on somethin' else.

"Nigga, just come on!" as we crossed the floor, there she was walking with her friends.

I said, "Say-say-say, baby! You in the purple! You like fat boys?"

I started beat boxin' and making sound effects. She'd glanced my direction but kept on strolling. "oh, so you don't hear me talkin' to you? You just gon' keep on walkin', huh? Emm-em-mmm! I'll eat it up!"

Brew stupid ass gone say, "Yo, you ever stop to think, that's exactly what she might be afraid of?"

His fool ass was laughin' and shit. I said, "Fuck you, I'm serious! My nigga, you see all that ass?" I questioned as we followed her and her squad.

He said, "Yeah, I see it, no doubt. But I also see somethin' else! Here comes Thomas, nigga. Turn your back and just walk," he warned me. Thomas runs his shit with an iron fist. He owns the club.

"Shit-shit-shit! Walk wit' me. You think he seen me?"

"I don't know. Ya ass ain't supposed to be in here. You all out in the open stylin' and shit. You buggin'!" I thought I was cool, until Thomas called my name.

23

"Terrence! Terrence, is that you?"

"Yup, he saw you. Just go, I'll hold 'em off..." I ducked off in the crowd while Brew so-called did his thing.

"Mr. Thomas, how you doin' today sir?"

"I'm doing fine, Ahmad. Is that, was that Terrence I just saw with you?"

"Uh, naw. Nope, you talkin' about fat Terrence?"

"Yeah, your boy Crook. He's not old enough to be in here yet. And look, if you're lying to me, I'll put the both of you out. Now, you wanna tell me the truth?" he asked. Little did he know, I wasn't old enough to be in the building, either. I'd used my brother's ID.

"Wait a minute now Mr. Thomas. Let's be reasonable. I ain't seen Croo— I mean Terrence. If he's here, I ain't got nothin' to do with it, sir."

"Oh yeah? You wanna lie, huh? Move around Ahmad. Enjoy what you can while it last. You won't be here much longer. Excuse me."

"Shit," I uttered.

He said, "I'll find him, then I'll be back for you."

I couldn't do shit but smile. He gave me his back and I dipped off. I saw Crook heading towards the bathroom. I had the munchies. I went to the closest bar and grabbed me some peanuts.

***

Fuck! Thomas just stepped in the midst of everybody. It's plenty people that ain't of age up in here. But he's lookin' for my ass and none other. I slid off the floor and went in the bathroom, hoping he hadn't spotted me. When I stuck my head out the door ten minutes later, Brew was standing to my right.

He said, "You know he huntin' for you right?"

"Yeah, I seen 'em. What he say? Stop chewin', nigga! What he say?"

"He said when he find yo' fat ass, both of us outta here because I lied to him."

"Damn, for real?" my heart dropped. "Is he still on the floor somewhere where you can see 'em?" I asked.

"Nah, he on the move. Just like yo' ass better be. I'm about to get out of here and grind on some of these asses and titties before he give us the boot. So, you're on your own for now."

"Brew! B-Brew!" he spun off.

I told myself fuck the dumb shit and came on out.

K'ajji

CHAPTER 7
WOULD YOU KNOW?

Out on the floor, The Basement Brothers slowed it down. I see my nigga and Honesty slow dancin'. Bella, Telesis, Wintress, and Yetta were even out there. Every nigga in there had a tender, or was in search of one, as Freddie Jackson sang *'You Are My Lady.'* I had to move fast before Thomas Alvin off the Cosby Show lookin' ass brought that Sandman from The Apollo. All my niggas was clutching hard! It's plenty ass and titties in this bitch, familiar and unfamiliar. The East and some are up in this shit. I've got a few dimes in the building, but I want something new. Lookin' around, I spotted cutty wearing the purple standing by the ladies' bathroom door about ten feet away from me.

I said, "Heeey!" as loud as I could, snappin' my fingers to the beat. I grooved, while looking her way. She noticed me gawking. She'd smiled and shook her head at my foolishness. That's all I'd needed to see was that smile. I slowly bopped my way over to her, as the DJ mixed in Surface's *Shower Me with Your Love*. When I got to her, I didn't say shit. I simply extended my hand as I mouthed, and lip sang the words. She took my hand. As we started boppin', I pulled her to me, extended her and spun her like my momma always taught me. As she came back in, I popped at her.

"So, what's your name sweetheart?"

She said, "It's definitely not *sweetheart*. And why? Who wanna know?"

Just as jazzy at the mouth, I answered, "Crook, baby. *Crook* wanna know."

"Crook, huh?" Her mouth curled into a frown. "My name Erneeka." She gave me half of a smile. "My friends call me Neeka."

"Where you from, Ms. Neeka? I ain't never seen you before."

"Cause we ain't from here." She replied.

"Aw, we huh? Where y'all from?"

"St. Louis." She lied.

I said, "Damn! No wonder you thicker than a piece of corn bread with butter, cheese and peppers! What brings you this way?" She said, "We're visiting my cousin, Octavia."
"Oct-tavi, what the hell? Don't even tell me. Negroes and these damn names. Let me guess, she was born in October, huh? That makes her a Scorpio or a Libra. It don't matter, they both crazy as hell."
She started laughing. "Shut up, boy! You can't be talking about cuz like that. Anyways, somebody like it. I see dude you were with earlier over there dancing wit' her. I gotta talk to her nasty self. Over there letting him feel on her booty and stuff." She frowned.
"Wha-where they at?" I looked around frantically. "Did I – did I say she was crazy? Damn, my bad."
"You funny. So, those the types of girls you like?" She stopped dancing.
"Hold up now. I'm just kiddin'. I'm looking at my type standin' in front of me right now."
"Em-hmm." She took my hand again. I pulled her off the floor.
She said, "And who is it that you're here with, Crook? 'Cause I'm seein' more than a few females lookin' at me kinda strange right now."
"They just curious. They ain't never seen you before, that's all."
"You sure you ain't got no girl up in here?"
"We good trust me. So, why you ain't answer me when I was tryin' to holla at you earlier?"
"Cause you rude."
"What, rude?"
"Yeah, you don't come at me like that. I heard you talkin' about my butt!" she laughed.
"Terrence!" Thomas tapped me on my shoulder.
Damn, I'm caught. Fuck! I thought.
"Tell her goodbye, Terrence!" he said, as I'd turned to face him.

CHAPTER 8
Proof

Outside in the parking lot of The Matrix, me, Congo, Big I and True sat in a black tinted Suburban. True is in the driver's seat.

B.I. said, "Here comes Shyla now. Roll the window down, this button ain't workin'. What these muthsfuckas got childproof on 'em or some shit? Come on, nigga! She right here."

"A'ight nigga, damn! It's unlocked." True replied. B.I. rolled his window down.

He said, "These niggas don't know me. I'm tellin' you. Shy, where my sister at?" he questioned.

She said, "Neeka up in there dancin' with one of them niggas y'all pointed out last week. She told me to come tell y'all what's up. She said it's a lot of guns up in there. I know the two dudes I danced with had one."

They in there, huh?" he nodded.

"Yeah, it's a bunch of niggas in there. All gangsters. Everybody shit banged to the right. I feel like an alien. I ain't use to this shit. You know? It's about to end any minute now."

He said, "A'ight. Tell sis I said get out. Y'all get up outta here now! Drive back to Chicago. I'll see y'all when I get there."

True said, "What the fuck you doin'? They comin' out. You don't see all them people? Roll that window up, nigga!"

"A'ight, hold up. Shy get everybody out. We gone hit the block and come back shootin'. Y'all can't be out here. Hurry up and leave."

BREW

The party was over. I saw Smoke and Thirty standing by the main exit talkin' to some bitches. I'm trying to run yang on one of the shorties from the Lou, in hopes of gettin' us all some pussy. The way I see it is, one go, they all goin'. That's until her friend or so-called cousin ran up on some straight hate, cock-blockin' shit while they were hugged up.

"Octavia, cuz we gotta go! Where Neeka at?" she said, pulling her arm. Brew pushed her hand away.

"Gon wit' that shit! Don't you see me and young love talkin' right here? Damn!" she'd grabbed Octavia's arm again, but this time she snatched away.

She said, "Hold on Shyla! Dang girl!"

"Octavia, bitch! Ooh!" Shyla got frustrated, but then remembered Octavia ain't know anything about what was going on.

She said, "Look Mya, you and Courtney stay here with Oct. Make sure this hoe don't move. Steph, you and Mi-Mi come with me. We gotta find Neeka. We gotta go! Be ready when we get back, Octavia, or we leavin' yo' ass! Where this bitch Neeka at? Neekaaa!" she yelled over the heads of everybody exiting as they maneuvered through the crowd coming towards them. Neeka was nowhere in sight.

CHAPTER 9
TWO MILES PER HOUR
Proof

The ride around the block seemed to take forever. But it was time to ride. The parking lot was lit up. Niggas was flossin', showing off their whips. Coming back around, there were a few cars pullin' out, but a lot of niggas were still standing around. I recognized a few Eastside niggas, as well as niggas from other areas. A few of 'em glanced at the truck but were too busy trying to get some pussy to realize that muthafuckas were about to die! Everybody with me knew what it was. B.I. had the pump ready, and Congo had two .357's. I cocked my nine. *God, grant me serenity. Will you accept me?* My heart has grown cold. And I couldn't change it. Slowly, the windows came down.
"Almighty! Wussup, niggaz!" I yelled, as I was first to open fire.

Brew

I was still runnin' it to shorty, hands full of nothin' but ass! Bro was hollering at her buddy when we heard shots outside. All hell broke loose. People started runnin', screamin', and gettin' trampled and shit. Shorty held me tight as everybody that had just left out, came flying back in. It was a full-blown stampede. Niggaz wit' thrillaz was scramblin' tryin' to get out there. All you heard were screams and, "They shootin'!"
I'm thinkin' one of the folks probably out there showin' out. Shootin' in the air or some shit. Then, somebody yelled, "Them Vice Lords outside!"
Lookin' around, I saw all mine who had been in the building except Crook. Then it dawned on me, Thomas had security put him out. Him and the lil' bitch he was talkin' to had to be outside. I pushed the broad up off me and upped.
She screamed.

K'ajji

I said, "Come mo' nigga," as I tugged at Freak's shirt. We headed for the door. "Thirty, Six, Smoke! Aye, get Tank! Y'all come mo'! Crook out there!" I pushed my way through the crowd blockin' the exit. "Move! Get the fuck outta here! Mooove!" We made it outside ready to dump shit down, but we were too late. The Hooks were gone, leaving plenty niggas stretched out in their wake. Dre Epps and a few more of the Folks were out there snappin' while females tended to the wounded and the dead.

As cars peeled out leaving the scene, my eyes scanned the lot. I saw ole girl in the purple standing next to one of the Regals lookin' like she was stuck. She stood there with both hands covering her mouth as she peered downwards in between the cars. I knew it couldn't have been good.

"Come on, y'all!" I yelled and we ran over to the whips.

What I saw put my heart in my stomach. "All n'aw! Not my nigga!" I kneeled down. Blood was everywhere. He had a big hole in his neck. Complete and the rest of 3C came out the building.

Honesty was calling for her man. "Six! Where Marcus at?" she cried.

I said, "Come on y'all. Let's pick 'em up and get 'em to a hospital."

Smoke closed his eyes and took his gun out of his hand. It was still smokin'. Smoke said, "It's too late. He gone."

"Muthafuckaz!" Six yelled at the top of his lungs, pacing back and forth wit' his thrilla in hand. Honesty spotted us and ran over to us, but he quickly wrapped his arms around her, shielding her. Though she tried, he wouldn't let her through.

She said, "What happened! Who is that? Who is that?" she sobbed. She had her .380 in hand.

Six whispering softly, he said, "It's Crook, bae. It's Crook, they shot 'em."

"Oh naw!" Honesty cried. Sirens could be heard in the distance.

Six said, "Come mo'. Ain't no need you seein' him like that. Let's get you back in the building. I told y'all to stay put."

Seconds later, the police pulled up blocking the lots exits.

Smoke said, "Here."

The Streets Will Never Close 3

I took his and Crook's guns.

He said, "Everybody go. Get back to the hood. I'll stay with him." As we walked off, he said, "Aye Brew, tell Six to get the girls out of here. Once they good, y'all go by bro momma crib. I'll get up wit' y'all at the hospital."

"A'ight, Treys! 3C, my nigga."

Walking back in the building, I could see the horror in every chick's face I made eye contact with. All the gangstas looked as if they were ready to kill somethin'. Tammy B raised hell. She's Telesis's auntie, and she was adamant about not letting any of the ladies from the deck leave out them doors with us. We had problems. Six wouldn't move until he was sure they'd get home safe. Tammy said she'd take 'em. They were all strapped, so I knew they were good. Though Tammy begged us to stay, we were out.

Crook's momma stayed on Brown. It was late. His big sister answered the door. She'd let us in as she'd always did, assuming Crook was with us. She gave us her back, walking towards the living room. We stepped in.

She said, "I'm startin' to hate you lost your key. Terrence, some girl named Aisha keep callin' here. You know mama—she'd turned to look for him.

Shit, I don't know if she'd seen the blood on my clothes, or the looks on our faces had given it away.

She fell to her knees and started screaming. "Terrence! Oh my God, where my brother? I told 'em! I told 'em not to go! I had a dream about this shit! Ma! Mama!" she screamed.

We heard her footsteps as she came down the stairs. Then there she was. Housecoat, facial cream and pink rollers in her head. She was rubbing her eyes, still half asleep. Crook's momma said, "Terrence! Terrence and Tamia, what the hell goin' on down here?"

33

K'ajji

CHAPTER 10
Po

Lord knows not hearing her voice in weeks was really startin' to fuck wit' me. When Kia opened her eyes, waking up from the medically induced coma, I was right there at her bedside.

"Bae, I'm here." I stroked her arm.

Blinking uncontrollably, she then fixed her gaze on the ceiling. The doctor stepped back.

Her mother, wheelchair bound began to pray out loud.

"Kia, you hear me?" I asked. She nodded, then turned her head slightly to her left to look at me. Taking her hand, I smiled. "What up? Damn say somethin'. How you feel? You a'ight?"

"Yeah, ahem!" she cleared her throat. "I need some water."

I looked at the doctor for approval as I reached for the pitcher. He nodded giving me the okay.

"Kia!" her mother called out. "Po y'all sat her up some more so I can see her."

I said, "Aigh't, hold up, Ma. I gotchu."

The doctor stepped in. "Ms. Thompson, hello I'm Dr. Ryan. Now that you're all done with your surgeries, I'll be taking care of you. I'm going to sit you up so your mother can see you and you can take in some water, okay?"

She nodded, as the bed began to rise.

"Hey baby!" her mother cried.

"Hey Ma." Kia replied in a sandy voice as tears raced down her face. I put the straw to her mouth, and she took a sip of water. Her eyes were different. She's traumatized.

Though I hated too rehash everything she'd went through, I had questions.

The doctor said, "Ms. Thompson, I want to begin our physical therapy sessions as soon as you're able. I'm going to give you guys the room. I know you have a lot of catching up to do. Young lady, if you feel any pain at all I want you to press that red button there at the bottom of your controller. There's also a menu here. Order some food. It's almost lunch time. We've been feeding you through tubes.

You should be well hydrated. It's time for some solid carbohydrates."

"I'll make sure she gets somethin'," I assured him. he stepped out. And right or wrong, I went straight in. "Kia what happened?" Who did this shit?'

She said, "I don't know. Some short, light-skinned dude I'd never seen before snatched me up at ZaZa's. He wasn't alone though. My face was covered the entire time, but I heard other voices. They said you'd know what this is about when I said 3C. They're looking for you and Ross."

It was the twins. The painful truth is this is my fault. A nigga gotta live with the facts in all his actions. I'd put deathly blows on Doe bitch and put her buddy in a coffin. The slugs I'd put in his chest hadn't stopped his heart, so he'd touched mine in return. Now I was feeling his wrath. Or was I? Had Proof figured out that it was me and Ross on his ass that night we hit his cousin at the gas station? How could I be sure this wasn't Zoo and his niggas? There was no way I could tell if this was a spin-off. Whichever the case may be, one thing was guaranteed. It was time to let niggas know Po back in this bitch!

"Why they find you naked?' I asked her.

Her mother said, "Yeah baby, what happened to your clothes? Did, did they..."

The tears got worse. Her entire body shook. She said, "Ma, they stuck-stuck guns inside mee! I was so scared!"

"Oh my God!" her mother yelled.

Picturing that shit fucked me up.

CHAPTER 11
Six

"It's been cold as a bitch all winter. Everything about today is wrong. We shouldn't be buryin' you dog. I barely made it here in time. Smoke was driving too slow. Can you see me? Blue button-up shirt, black dress pants, tie and loafers. Your church service is over. It's time to put you in the ground. Rollin' you outta the hearse, I can't believe we're here again. They took the air from your lungs so young. Before fathers, we're Pallbearers. We got chu, my nigga. My feet slidin' because it snowed a lil' bit last night, that's all. I ain't gon' drop you.

When you carry one of your best friends to his final resting place, it stays with you forever. This shit's hard, and beyond scary. In fact, it's one of the hardest things I've had to do."

"Ye though I walk through the valley of the shadow of death, I will fear no evil. For thou art with me, thy rod and thy staff they comfort me." We'd set him down.

As the Reverend did his thing, I walked over to the immediate family and hugged his mother first, then his sister. Looking over Tamia's shoulder, seeing the pain in Yetta's face, I grabbed her as well. Crook was her lil' cousin, so I knew she was just as fucked up as the rest of us right now.

Eyes red-rimmed, I could tell she was all cried out. I imagine my eyes are demon red as well. They're barely open. We blew damn near a zip before we left my crib this morning. My high was short lived. Suddenly I heard the darkness of gunfire ringing out. Instinctively, I pushed Yetta, Ms. Taylor and Tamia to the ground, using my body to shield them from the terror as slugs pierced the line of cars in front of us.

Several long seconds passed before the bullets storm paused. I was able to stagger to my feet. Grittin' my teeth, I pulled the two nines from my waistband in search of my target. I saw the outline of the chopper as flames blazed from the barrel hanging out the window of a silver Bronco. Shuffling backward, I opened up spittin'

K'ajji

bullets at the lone gunman perched in the back of the truck as he let off a continuous burst of rounds from his rifle.
Bak! Bak! Bak! Bak! Bak! Bak! Bak! Bak! Bak! Bak!
I let the nine—double M's bark, as they sped toward the cemetery's exit. To my left, I saw Moo, Doe, Smoke and Telesis sending echos of war as well. I could only wish all of this was a dream, but, shit was real.

CHAPTER 12
Wintress

Damn, this hurts like hell! My stomach is on fire! I—I wanna see it, but Doe keep whispering in my ear, telling me not to look.
"It's just a scratch. You good. You gon' be a'ight. Just be still and stay with us. Breathe."
Why does he keep saying the same thing over and over? It must be bad. I feel like I swallowed a piece of hot metal. I ain't never been shot before. Beyond my own groans, I hear moans and screams. I hear Yetta yelling at the top of her lungs, beggin' me to get up. I wish I could, but I can't. Every time I try to move my arms to touch where it hurts, Doe pushes my hands away and holds me a little tighter. This copper taste of blood in my mouth is hideous. My ass is freezing! It feelslike an icicle. Maybe that is why I can't feel my legs.
"Mm-ma. Mama! Momma!" I called out under my breath.
"Shhhh!" Doe hushed me. "We gon' get chu to the hospital first."
Underneath all the G-shit, I was still vulnerable inside. My momma gon' be pissed about me being late picking her up from work.
"Moo, say somethin'. What we doin'?" Doe questioned in an unstable voice.
Telesis walked over and looked down at me. Black fur and black dress on. The black Glock resting in her hand with its cylinder sittin' back, she wore a face of stone.
Tears blackened by her mascara, she said, "Hold on, Win. Help is on the way."
I felt like nothin' could stop this burnin'. Over Yetta and the other's screams, I could hear Moo giving his decree.
Then, the sound of sirens. The pitch seems different this time. What I'd always fled from, sounds more like mythical horns from some far away land. I'm a little girl again. I saw me in my room playing with dolls imagining this princess fairytale.

K'ajji

Like an unworldly magical assemblance of chariots coming to my rescue at this alarming sound by horse. Then, I was back here again, laying on this cold ground bleeding. Now, I saw white people. Maybe this was what my mother always spoke on. God, am I dying? Is this what it feels like? Is death coming? What is this drowsiness I feel upon me right now? I-I just wanna close my eyes for a minute. Just a minute. Maybe this pain will go away.

CHAPTER 13
Telesis

Zig zagging at a high speed, the truck tore up the narrow pathway and darted into traffic. In a trance, I glared over the sight of my thriller until the threat was no longer visible. All the gunfire ceased, leaving a smell of gunpowder and hot metal lingering in the air. Trembling, I lifted my gaze from the graveyard's exit and lowered my strap. Looking back, a warped silence I'd never felt before fell upon me. The images played in my mind like a horror movie. My eyes welled up as I desperately searched the faces of the wounded. Thank God they were still alive.

My heart's rhythm thumped out of control. I saw pooling, and blood splattered wildly across the thin two inches of snow, causing some to melt. To see it streaming along the pavement like a spilled glass of wine did something to me. Coming out of my zone, I could suddenly hear again. Screaming in agony from their injuries, some crawled while others rolled from side to side on their backs and bellies in reaction to the slugs.

"Wintress!" I yelled, shaking my head, swallowing some of my salty tears.

She was one of many caught in the crossfire. Her arms flopping at her side, her gun laid at her feet. Trying to see the wound in her stomach for herself, Doe was doing his best to hold her still as he cradled her upper body in his lap.

"Win! Win-Wintress, get up!" Yetta cried, tears choking her words.

Honesty had to restrain her. She was going crazy about her best friend. Moo limped over to me, suppressing the pain.

He had a bullet hole in his thigh.

"You a'ight?" he asked, eyebrows raised. He stared at the empty trusty Glock in my right hand.

"What the hell!" I pressed my lips together, trying to stop the tears. "Am I a'ight?" I smirked. "You the one bleedin'."

He said, "I know right." He nodded to my right.

Crossing my arms, I tucked the nine under my armpit as I looked and took notice at the Reverend and a few women from the church staring my direction. I rolled my eyes at 'em, I leaned back against my car.

I said, "Fuck 'em. We gotta worry about you and everybody else out here hit."

He said, "That was Po and nem!" He clenched his jaw, slumped over and took a knee in front of me. "I'm good." He smiled wickedly.

He said, "Lesis, we gotta get everybody to the hospital. Get in. Pop your trunk real quick."

I said, "Boy, you ain't gettin' or puttin' nobody in my damn trunk. What's wrong with you?"

"I know, just do it." Swinging my door open, I got in and did as he'd asked.

He yelled, "Doe, Six! Everybody with a thrilla, hand that shit over. Y'all know the police comin'! Throw them joints in here!" He looked over at the Reverend, the Pastor and the rest of the Church goers. "Y'all ain't see nothing, right?"

They all shook their heads, as 3C fell in line to drop their weapons in the trunk.

Moo said, "Lesis, you know what it is."

Looking me directly in my eyes, he yelled, "Yetta, come here!"

Seeing she was the most troubled, he wanted her gone.

"Moo-Moo, I ain't leavin' Win-Wintress! I-I can't!" she cried.

He got up, hobbled over there and grabbed her. "Girl, bring yo' ass here!" He snatched her to her feet. "You ain't doin' shit but scaring her! All that hollerin' and shit!" He told her, as he dragged her by the arm.

Opening my passenger side door, he shoved her inside and closed her in.

"We ain't got time for this shit! We gon' get her some help! Chill the fuck out! Pull off, Lesis, she goin' with you. Y'all know what to do. Go to the spot on Brown when it's done. We'll call through there in about an hour." I pulled off.

CHAPTER 14
Doe

When the shots rang out and I looked up, the first thing I noticed was the silver Bronco. We'd ran across it at one of Ross's spots during our search for him some weeks back. Moo being hit, I'd definitely have to bring the heat to 'em in our quest for revenge. The police fucked around and pulled up before the ambulance. Underhanded, redneck muthafuckas didn't give a fuck who lived or died. They laid everybody down alongside the wounded. Fifteen had been hit. Seven of ours, five family members and three from the church. Honesty got out of there with a few of ours, but I don't wanna try to move Wintress. Bullets traveled and I didn't wanna cause more damage.

"Can't y'all see all these people out here bleedin'! We need some help out here! Get us some muthafuckin' help!" I yelled, as they pulled me away from her. Laying me on my stomach, they put me in cuffs.

"Wintress, you gon' be a'ight! Just stay calm!" She looked as if she was about to pass out. "Look at me, Win! Just stay calm. Breathe with me. Look, look! No, eye to eye, Win!"

"Help is on the way, sir," a yellow-haired female officer announced standing over me with one of her feet in the middle of my back.

"We're gonna need cones and some evidence bags out here! We've got a lot of different casings. Semi-automatic!" I heard one Cop tell the others as he slowly paced across the snow carpeting the grass.

"Okay, where are the guns?" A male's voice firmed up behind me.

"We're gonna check every vehicle out here, until we find them!" another proclaimed.

Moo yelled, "Ain't no guns out here, dog! Damn! Somebody did a drive-by on us!"

"And by the looks of things, somebody shot back. Safety first ladies and gentlemen. Give up the guns."

Finally, the EMTs pulled up. They'd scooped Wintress up first and like a bloodhound on the trail of a wanted fugitive, Gina pulled up as well. She hopped out of the Crown Victoria and flashed her gold shield as they were wheeling Wintress into the back of the bus on a stretcher.

"Hold up!" She stopped the paramedics. "That's Wintress Knight. How is she? Whatchu got?"

"Bullet wound to the abdomen. Through and through," one of the EMT's announced. "Got her pretty good. She's critical. Gotta go."

"Okay, go! Get her and the rest of these people to a hospital. Who's in charge?" she asked. "What in God's name! Girrl, if you don't get your foot off that boy's back!"

"We were first on the scene. No one is dead. What's your interest here detective?" A short, bald, white dude asked her. He was wearing a black shirt with *GANG UNIT* scrawled across the back. Two more in the same gear stood at his side.

Gina said, "I heard a few familiar names come across the scanner. Where they go, bodies tend to follow."

"And what names might that be?" one of the bald guy's partners asked, twirling a set of cuffs.

"Ooh, no he didn't." Gina rolled her neck. She said, "Moozeere and Domain, y'all ain't properly introduce y'all selves to these people?" At least she'd smiled when she said it. "Y'all don't know who the twins are?"

Baldy said, "I know exactly who they are." Stepping in for his colleague as they rolled Moo by on a rack.

"She said, "Okay, you've been briefed. Y'all actin' as if you're new to the force." She held up one finger. "Hold on. Moo, they popped you too, huh? I'll see you at the hospital." She turned her attention back toward the officers. "And whether y'all like it or not, this one is coming with me." She reached down and grabbed me by my arm. "Doe, come to your knees for me. I'm gonna lift you up on the count of three. One, two!" They gave her no argument as I stood to my feet. "What did y'all find?" she asked.

44

The officer collecting evidence said, "Nothing. A bunch of spent casings so far."
"A shootout?" she questioned.
"I'm certain," he replied.
She said, "Well, don't waste your time. You won't find any weapons out here. Reverend Jeffs, Pastor Harper y'all see anything?"
They both looked at me and said no.
"Sisters, what about y'all? Y'all see what happened out here?"
They denied seeing anything as well.
"Am I under arrest?" I asked.
She said, "Nall, not yet. But I'ma take you in and check your hands for gunpowder residue. If somebody wind up dead, I'll know you were one of my shooters." She turned and began walking me to her car.
I said, "Bella, y'all make sure everybody straight at the hospital until I can get there!"

K'ajji

CHAPTER 15
Gina

Giving them my back as I walked Doe to my car, I heard one of guys from the Gang Unit mumble, "I betcha she's dirty."
It gave me pause. I stopped, but didn't turn around.
Another officer overheard the comment and came to my defense, "Gina? Never."
I smiled. While he's talkin' shit I should have IA take a hard look at that ass. I kept it moving. Some of us got work to do. After easing Domain in the back, I got in and drove off leaving the cemetery. As we rode through local traffic, I tried him as we stopped at a streetlight.
"You wanna holla at me now? Or you wanna wait until we get to the station?" I glanced at him through my rearview.
Staring at me, I could barely see the whites of his eyes. "You can pretend like you don't hear me all you want. Keep it up! You and yo' crazy ass brother gon' find y'all selves surrounded by bricks and barbed wire fences."
The light turned green. He looked daggers at me until I hit the gas.
He said, "Ain't that a bitch?" He looked out of the window.
"Whatchu just say, boy! You talkin' to a woman! You should know anything with the word bitch in it is out the window. Don't disrespect me! I'll take this badge off and get on that witcha."
"Whatever happens, happens!" he replied.
"Domain, believe it or not. Ever since y'all started comin' of age, I've been tryin' to warn y'all about the shit storm of trouble a life of crime can land y'all in. Open your eyes! Somebody just tried to off y'all at a fuckin' funeral! Crook momma couldn't even bury her son in piece! Y'all ready to die! For what? Can you even tell me?"
"Nah." He smiled. "I can't tell you shit. You know it all, Ms. Detective. You just tryin' to help, right?" He gave me this demurring look.

"Yeah, that's right! And y'all can't expect me to turn a blind eye to this game. Y'all out here playin' God! You, Moo and all y'all little proteges! Where y'all think y'all goin' in this fast lane y'all in? If puttin' you in prison will save your life, or somebody else's, so be it."

We'd pulled up to the precinct. Leaning forward, he tilted his head to the side.

"Now you're being very disrespectful. Before I let you give me a L—Ball, I'm goin' all out! You wanna cage me like some animal! Two niggas trapped in a cell smaller than your bathroom!"

He shook his head. "That ain't livin'."

"Is that what your father told you? Or was it Moo? Mind you being dead ain't living either. Ain't nothin' nobody can do for you then, but cry and drop a rose in the hole on yo' ass!"

I got out, looped around the hood of the car and pulled him out as well.

He said, "I don't know what you brought me all the way down here for. Ain't shit happenin'."

"Aw, it's a lot happenin'. Believe that." It was a long shot, but I had to try to push his buttons. I really didn't have shit on them, but a hunch. I walked his ass in, right past my desk, toward the interrogation room. "I got one for GSR testing! Shootout at the cemetery!"

"Any dead?" Jamison questioned, sitting at his desk eating an oversized burger.

"I don't know. Hold up, Domain. Stand right here—" We paused. I went back to my desk, opened the drawer and grabbed my Murder Book. "Where mine at?" I asked eyeing Jamison's sandwich.

"Burke, you hungry?" he yelled, as I escorted Domain into interrogation.

"Just bring me a kit, Jamison! Hold still, Doe." I removed the handcuffs. "Now sit down."

He took a seat in the chair.

I threw the photo album on the table in front of him. I took pleasure in opening it for him. This particular file held all the pictures of the dead drug dealers I'd pegged them as being responsible for. Sliding the pictures out, I'm sure he saw all my post-it notes. They read, The Twins, Moo-Moo and Doe-Doe. A.T.K./3C. They were stuck to the top of numerous pictures.

"I know you remember this one. When y'all ran up in Tre-Rida spot dressed like Freddy?" He frowned. "Or how about this one? The murder y'all just did up on Burleigh, killing Joseph Wales McKinnley?" He laughed from his soul.

He said, "You don't know what the fuck you talkin' about lady! Ahhh-ha-haaaa!"

"Oh, you think it's funny? What about this one. Moo was locked up for it, but I know this will jog your memory. I slid the picture of four different people in front of him, with his name alone scribed in red at the top of each of them. "You caught these two dudes coming out of the movie theater with these two young ladies. These two here, Seneca and Key were in the streets. But why kill the girls they were with?"

"You done?" he asked, still wearing a smile.

"I just wanna know—"

"Nah, for real! You done?"

"Domain, I—"

"Lawyer!" He folded his arms in front of him. "I don't know nothin' about none of this shit you talkin', Gina! Call my attorney and holla at him. His name is—"

"I know. Robert Henak."

He said, "And, y'all ain't swabbin' shit until he gets here."

I said, "Damn, it's like that? You had so much to say in the car. I'm on that ass, huh?" He just sat there smiling. I gathered my things and stepped out of the room.

Jamison said, "I saw the interview. Time to cut him loose."

I said, "Yeah, I know. Kick him loose but put a tail on him. They're gonna be out for blood tonight and I'm tired of this shit."

"Will do," Jamison replied. "Besides, another call just came in. You've got three down on Burleigh."

CHAPTER 16
Jah

I was trying to get some work around the house done. Potpourri burned lightly on the stove, I had Michelle's *Something in My Heart* flowing from the Kenwood. Coming out of the laundry room with my clothes in tow, Doe walked in with his tuxedo covered in blood. Dropping the basket, I damn near lost my mind.

"Doe-Doe what happen! Whose blood is that?"

"Win's," he replied. He'd barely looked up at me as I followed his ass into the bedroom.

"Wha-what's goin' on!" I asked, as he opened the closet.

"Moo and a bunch of other people got hit, too."

"*Whatchu mean got hit?* Got hit where? Was y'all fightin'?" I questioned as he threw a hangered outfit across the bed. He grabbed the mini-Sentry safe where he kept a few guns.

I thought, *God, please don't let this boy tell me somebody else is dead.*

He said, "At the funeral. Niggas shot that joint up."

We still hadn't made eye-contact, which was never a good sign. I hated when he got like this, because no matter what I said, he didn't listen. I went and looked out of the bedroom window to see who, if anybody was outside. I hadn't heard the bass growl I'd grown accustomed to hearing when him, or niggas from his team pulled up. All I saw was a blue Ford Taurus creep by. It looked like the police.

"What? They a'ight? The police just rode by starin' at the house!"

"I don't know." he replied. "Moo straight. Wintress looked pretty bad." He started taking his clothes off. "I need you to getcha brothers on the phone while I go hop in the shower." Stripping down to his boxers, he tried to head for the bathroom.

I stepped in front of him blocking the doorway. "You ain't goin' nowhere." I made him look at me.

"Come on, Jah, watch out." He brushed me to the side.

"Wait a damn minute! Ho—how you get here? I don't see—"

51

Marching past me, I was now talking to his muscular back. He still hadn't looked me in my eyes.

He said, "I walked. I had to clear my head. Them bitches followed me."

"Wha-what bitches?" I asked as I perused him down the hallway.

"The police." He turned and stopped me at the bathroom door. I finally saw his eyes, and he saw mine. "Look no more questions, bae. Call them niggas. I gotta holla at 'em. Please, just do as I ask. Don't worry about nothin'. I'll be out in a minute."

He shut the door. Engrossed in the pain I heard in his voice. I went and made the call. When he got out of the shower ten minutes later, my brothers were on the line. I handed him the phone and listened intently to what he'd had to say.

He said, "Hello? Wassup, my niggas? Shit, hot as a bitch right now. I just got outta the shower. Aye, y'all remember that crib we was lookin' to purchase out on 33rd. Yeah, yup the one with the big bay windows. The realtor back in town. She ready. They got at us today. A few hours? A'ight, call that number I gave y'all when y'all get here. For sure, I'll tell her." He hung up. "Your brothers said they love you. They'll see you when they get here. Oh, yeah, I'ma need your car."

"For what? What y'all up to, Doe—Doe!"

"Nothin'." He smiled. "I need some lotion. Where you put it?"

"You know I can tell when you lyin' right? You make me sick."

CHAPTER 17
Yetta

We're over a hundred strong in this two-story Victorian house. It was six in the evening by the time Doe made it to us at the spot on Brown. As he told us how Gina took him down to the 7th District Precinct and pulled it on him, my mind was elsewhere.

Though we'd received updates from the hospital saying everybody was in stable condition, I wanted to be there. I knew Win needed to see my face, just as I needed to see hers. We were all strapped, ready to go out there, but the police kept riding through.

"These hoes been followin' me all day!" Doe seethed, as he peeked out the curtain.

"Where else you go?" I asked.

He said, "I walked to Jah's when I left the police station."

I said, "Damn, you walked all the way out there? Why you ain't call nobody?"

He said, "I had to get myself together. I went out there, changed and grabbed her car. I rode around for a while trying to shake these fags, then went by Tipp's and jumped in the M.C. I thought I was trippin' until I got to Jahnahdah's and they was still on me."

Brew said, "You think they gon' hit us?"

He said, "For what, too many cars being parked outside?"

I said, "Damn, Twin. I wanna go to the hospital! I can leave this gun here."

He said, "Nah, you ain't leavin' shit. I'd rather you get caught with it, than without it. Bella and Honesty 'nem out there. Just chill for a minute. Let me think. When Moo say he was gon' call back?" he questioned.

Telesis said, "At seven. They tryin' to keep him over night. But you know better than anybody how stubborn that brother of yours can be."

"So, that was Ross and that nigga Po, huh?" Smoke asked, as he took a puff of the weed we had in rotation.

Doe said, "Yeah, that's right. But trust me, you lil niggas ain't gotta worry about it. It'll be taken care of. All we've been waitin' on was for the nigga to show his head."

"We feel you. Just know we ready to ride, my nigga," Six replied, holding an AK-47. "I'll go up in the attic and let this bitch fly at the jakes right now if you want me to."

"Hell nah, fool." Doe smiled shaking his head. "Then we'll never make it out of here. I didn't wanna stop, but I'm waiting on a call or two. They gotta do a shift change. We gon' wait it out."

He walked over and hugged my head to his stomach as I sat on the couch. "Yetta, we'll head to the hospital in the morning, a'ight, love?"

"I guess." I sucked my teeth. I was pissed!

The phone rang, and Thirty answered it, "Doe, it's for you."

Doe went over and grabbed it. "What's up? Oh, y'all made it—" There was a slight pause before he continued, "As much as I'd love to join y'all, I-I can't move right now. Go head, though. Yeah, I'm positive. Just hit me when y'all get it."

CHAPTER 18
Lil Davin

11:02 p.m.

Easing into the driveway, we came to a stop but the engine was still running. Sitting in the passenger's seat to my right, my brother pulled his mask over his face. Checking his gun for the last time, he was ready.

He said, "A'ight, nigga. You know what time it is. Gon' up there. Do it just like we do it at the crib, and we in." I laughed.

"Fuck is so damn funny! You ready?" I could tell his teeth were clenched under the rubber false face.

"You a white nigga! Big-ass nose." I giggled after thumping the tip of the synthetic rubber snot box and it recoiled back straight.

"Blood, stop playin' and take yo' ass up there. You know where I'm at." He slid out of the car.

Staying low to the ground, he ran on side of the house. Once he was in position, I casually got out and walked up on the front porch of the residence. Checking my surroundings, I rung the bell.

After a few seconds, the porch light came on. An old lady came to the door and looked out.

"Who is it?" she yelled.

I smiled innocently and gave her a friendly wave. "It's David, is Ravin here?"

Tucking my head slightly between my shoulders, as if I were freezing to death, I crossed my arms. I purposely hadn't worn a coat.

She said, "Lord, have mercy!"

The curtain on the door close, and I heard the locks clicking. As soon as the door cracked, I kicked that bitch sending Ross's mother flying backward.

Bro rushed in first wearing all black and the President Nixon mask, as I reached in my back pocket and grabbed Reagan. Pulling it over my skull, I stepped in, closed the door and upped the foe-five as his mother screamed.

"Stay down and shut the fuck up!" Bro barked standing over her with the pump. Tears sprang to her eyes.

"What's goin' on! I-I—"

"Bitch I said shut up!" Bruh kicked her in her stomach. His daughter came running down the stairs.

"Grandma, what was tha—" When she saw us, she tried to run back upstairs.

I caught her ass. She let out hackled screams as I dragged her down the stairs by her ankle, her head impacting every step. She was beautiful. About twenty-three with long hair and the body of a goddess, light-skinned with full lips. My type! I wish we could've met on better terms and different circumstances, but we're here on business.

Bro said, "This ain't about neither one of y'all! Just shut the fuck up. Do everything we tell y'all, and you might live!"

"Wh-wh-what do y'all want?" his mother cried.

I said, "Ms. Ross, it's time to see how far this love shit really goes." I grabbed her granddaughter by her hair and raised my gun to her temple. "We want you to call your son."

CHAPTER 19
Eric

"What the fuck? Stay focused, nigga!" I told myself inside. Because, in the midst and majesty of the moment it's most definitely the wrong time for the endorphins to be flowin'.

Standin' here with the sawed-off Bulldog aimed at this old lady, I still can't help but to notice the fine cheeks on Ross's daughter.

I thought, *Damn! The twins mentioned her being pretty, but that was a big understatement. Baby got back, too!*

"I kno-know the combination!" Ravin cried. "Just take the money and go!"

"*Combination?* What combination?" her grandmother asked.

"To-to th-the safe," she replied through her tears.

I looked at lil' bruh, looking at me and he shrugged.

"What chu think, Milhous?" he asked, calling me by Nixon's middle name.

I said, "I don't know yet. Where this safe at?"

"Up—upstairs in my room. G-Ma, I know I should've told you, but he' told me not to. I-I'm sor-rrry!" Ravin cried.

I said, "Nah, just make the call. We'll get to the money when he gets here."

Bro said, "Hold up, Richard! I'm the sittin' president! I think. I should be the one making the executive decision right now. I say, we should bundle that shit up to go real quick."

Fuck the dumb shit."

"We ain't here for that, Ronald!" I shook my head. I could tell his fool-ass was smiling though he was wearing a mask. I could hear it in his voice.

He said, "You serious right now?" He cocked his head to the side.

He let go of Ravin's hair and stood up.

I said, "A ight, fuck it. Take her up there and grab that shit. And hurry the hell up. Make sure you keep an eye on her, and not all that ass she got back there."

She mugged me.

"I got this," he replied. "A'ight Ravin, get up. Let's go! Show me where the money at." She got up. He said, "That muthafucka fat! How a fat ugly nigga make something so beautiful?" He walked her up the stairs with his gun in her back. "Yo' momma gotta be a bad bitch."

"Hurry up, nigga!" I barked as they disappeared.

Ross's mother was in pain. She was just lyin' there shuddering as she gazed into the darkness of my eyes behind the disguise.

"Just relax," I told her. "We just want you to call your son so we can holla at him. Erry-thang gon' be a'ight. After that, we outta here. Y'all can go back to livin' y'all—what the fuck!"

In the middle of me telling her they'd be able to go back to living their lives, I was interrupted by a gun blast. Seconds later, bruh came runnin' down the stairs. He was damn near falling down the steps dragging a duffle bag.

"What happened!"

He said, "I-I shot her!"

Her grandma shrieked from her soul to God.

"What! Why would you—"

"She pulled a gun on me!" he replied. "I got the money. Look."

"Where the fuck she get a gun from, huh? She ain't have shit on but a night gown!"

"It— it was tucked under some of the stacks of money!"

"N-o-o-o-o! Ra—vinnnn!" her grandmother screamed.

I put the barrel to her ribs. "Old lady, I swear fo-Jesus! Shut-shut cho ass up! Bruh, she dead?"

"Hell yeah. We gotta go!"

"You sure?" I asked.

"She gone, nigga."

"Damn, I told you to watch her!" I shook my head.

"No, please don't!" Ross's mother pleaded.

I aimed the shotty at her she laid balled up in the fetal position trying to cover her head.

"I'm sorry," I told her.

Pulling the trigger twice, I blew her insides against the wall. "I knew I shouldn't have let you take yo ass up there with that woman!" I scolded lil bruh.

"It ain't my fault, that bitch—"

"Just bring yo' ass on! Can't do nothin' right." We got up outta there.

K'ajji

CHAPTER 20
Moo

Layin' in the hospital the next morning, I turned on the TV. Coverage about the shootout at the cemetery and Ross's family being killed was all over the news. Somewhere in our grand scheme of things, shit went bad. I wondered what happen? Guess I'll find out soon enough. I just talked to Doe. They're on their way here now. I heard a faint tap at the door, before she'd stuck her head in.

"Moozeere?" Angie and her friend Trina appeared as she pushed the door open.

"Aw, damn. What's up?" I smiled but grimaced a little as I sat up.

"What y'all doin' here?" I asked, as they walked in letting the door close behind them. I turned the TV off.

Angie said, "We heard what happened, so I had to come check on you."

"So, you checkin' for me now?" I joked.

She said, "Don't let your head swell up bigger than it already is. It ain't like that." She was frontin' in front of company.

I said, "Yeah, right, whatever. Trina, what's up? You good?" She hadn't said shit.

She was just standing there looking as if she was surveying the room. They were both lookin' and smellin' so mutha-fuckin' good!

Trina said, "My bad, wassup, Moo. I wanna use your bathroom."

I said, "Go head. It's right there."

She said, "But first, let me tell you. I don't know what's up with your little security detail out there, or who she thinks she is! They got a mirror in there?"

"I'm pretty sure they do. Who you talkin' about, though? Honesty, Telesis or Bella?" I laughed.

She said, "That bitch Bella! Do you know she had the nerve to frisk us?" She frowned. "Put her hands all in my hair and stuff!"

She crossed her arms. "Talkin' 'bout she had to make sure I didn't have no razors."

I said, "She was just fuckin' with you."
"Nall, I think she's just mad a bitch is cuter than she is." She sucked her teeth. "Tell him, Angie!"
Angie said, "She did go a lil overboard."
I said, "It definitely ain't got nothin' to do with looks. Hold on now. You fine, but Bella nice, too!"
"Anyway." She waved me off and headed in the bathroom. Angie popped me upside my forehead.
"You do see me standin' here, right?" She rolled her eyes.
"You ain't checkin' for me, remember? I can have an opinion." I chuckled.
She said, "Um-hmm. You a trip."
"Nah, you a trip." I smiled. "Where the hell you been? It takes a nigga to catch a hot one to see you?"
She said, "It ain't even—"
"Like what?" I finished her sentence. "Let me guess. Like that?"
She whispered, "I've been around, I've just been busy, shoot. You know how it is."
I said, "You right. I know exactly how it is." As Trina came out of the bathroom questioning what we were whispering about, there was another knock at the door. I yelled, "We don't want none!"
Pushing the door open, Doe said, "Love you, too! What's uuuppp!" He ran in and hopped on the bed.
"Ah, watch my leg, fool!" I flinched.
Everybody flooded in. Hood, her crew, Tank, Six, Thirty and Brew. Angie took it as being their cue.
She said, "A'ight, Moozeere, I just wanted to make sure you were good. Call me, okay?"
I said, "Ho—hold on. Y'all just got here." She just smiled, grabbed Trina by her hand and headed for the door. "Aye, A.B., wait a minute." She turned, smiled, waved and they made their exit.
"*Aye, A.B., wait a minute!*" Hood mimicked me, as she wrapped her arms around me.
"Shut up." I smiled, hugging her back happy to see her.
Doe said, "Damn, she sounded just like you, too. Beggin' ass."
Everybody laughed, so did I.

The Streets Will Never Close 3

"How Win down there doin'?" I asked. "She fightin'?" Tank said, "Yeah, and we prayin'. She's still unconscious, but stable. The doctors say she'll pull through."

Doe said, "She's a soulja. I was worried for a minute. I thought we were gonna lose her. She got her mother, Yetta and some of the squad visiting her now."

"Moo, when you comin' home?" Hood asked.

I said, "Soon, I'm about ready to break up out this bitch."

She said, "And you in trouble, too. Teague said come straight to the house. He beatin' yo' ass for gettin' shot at a funeral."

"Tell Teague, I said he better be ready to pop me again. I ain't takin' no ass whippings. I saw the news. Three hit on Burleigh after the funeral?"

"Not us," Doe replied.

"Ross's family?" I asked.

Bruh said, "We'll talk when you get out of here. You know today is Pop's birthday, right?"

I said, "Yeah, I spoke to him last night. What he doin?"

"He flew out to Vegas," Hood replied. "Said, he needed some time away for a minute. He'll only be gone for a few days. You know what that means?" She bounced her shoulders, doing her little dance. "Time to party!" She smiled.

"With who!" me and Doe asked in unison.

She said, "With P.Y.T.! Dang, who y'all think? Both of y'all need to chill. Fa-real though."

K'ajji

CHAPTER 21
Po

Before his death, Congo, Spree and Kane were three of my mentor's closest allies. Besides me and Ross, J.L.'s trust didn't linger too much further in men. With five niggas, I knew we couldn't possibly win a war with 3C or Burleigh's youngins. So, in confidence that niggas would roll with me, I decided I'd start puttin' gatherings together, just for the O.G.'s from the Zoo. Today's meeting was the first of many to come. Nothin' but the old school.

"I open in saying, it's a sad day. We still don't know exactly who killed J.L. yet. And, as you all know, somebody killed folk's momma and his baby girl last night." I searched the eyes of everybody sitting at the table, as well as those standing along the walls before I continued, "Ross couldn't be here today. Because as we speak, and though he's grieving, he had to make funeral arrangements."

"It's been a whole lot going on. Damn, we ain't got no idea who's behind it?" Spree asked.

I said, "That's a good question. I'm glad you asked. I found out 3C was behind the incident with Kia. But this shit with Ms. Ross and Ravin is something else. Personally, I believe it was some of our own." Naturally, my words caused a lot of disorder.

"What the fuck you mean our own!" Congo roared over all the argumentation in the air.

Everybody felt him. I held up my hand to quiet them down. Soon, their voices came down to a bunch of whispers and I held their attention again.

"I mean exactly what I just said, my nigga. They made it look like a robbery, but this was a hit! Part of a hostile takeover.

A takeover orchestrated by none other than Lil Zoo," my words here also caused an uproar.

"Hell nah!" Kane shook his head like many others. "Po, you done lost yo' damn mind?"

"Oh, y'all don't see him tryin' to push us out?"

K'ajji

"Push who out!" Qubiah yelled as she mugged me. "I grew up with that boy's momma! Y'all do remember Chaka, right!"

I said, "You gon' go meet his momma you keep actin' dumb. And he gon' send you! Think! Who's in charge of everything now that he took over? How many of y'all got a block, or still runnin' your own spot in here?" Shit got quiet. "Nobody?" I continued. "Out of thirty five grown ass niggas and twenty-seven women, ain't nobody runnin' shit?"

"Nall, but Zoo said we'll still—"

I said, "Yeah, I heard 'bout that Tyra! But y'all can't be that stupid. If you ain't puttin' in no work, why would he pay you? Does that make any sense to you? Y'all think y'all collectin' SSI! Some kind of retirement benefits or some shit!" I laughed.

She rolled her eyes and sighed. "Nall, but I better get my money. Hell, I got three kids and bills to pay."

Every woman in the room cheered on what she'd said.

"Yeah, I hear y'all. But you better get yours or what?" I stood up and walked around the table. "What chu gon' do? This is the question I pose to all y'all."

Spree said, "Po, that's Jay family. He's left him the throne. What chu expect us to do?"

After the noise settled again, I said, "That's true. And as much love and respect I had for the late great John LeVon, I expect you to live. This is Zoo's reign, but I say we dethrone him. We go to war and take what's rightfully ours! The same should happen here as it would in any other kingdom where the king killed, overtaxed, and oppressed his people. As always, when there is treachery and anarchy amongst us, there shall be death. We built this shit! Y'all wanna eat, or you wanna starve?"

Congo said, "Let's eat!" I looked at Qubiah. I knew her decision would stand firm with the rest of the ladies.

She said, "Nigga, I'm always hungry." She gave me that smile of hers.

I said, "In the name of his mother, a true queen! We'll call this rebellion, Zulu! It's on!"

CHAPTER 22
Teague

Now being held here in Milwaukee County Jail on the charge of First-Degree Murder, police began investigating the alleged criminal activity of Corteague "Atkinson Teague" Phillups two years ago.

"Aye, big homie, ain't this you on TV?" Billion asked.

"Say, young blood! Turn that up." I stood up, as the news reporter continued.

She was standing outside the County Jail in the rain.

"He's been identified as a heavy Heroin distributor in the city. The Metro Drug Unit, FBI and Milwaukee Branch of the United States Drug Enforcement Administration provided additional assistance. They relied heavily on wiretaps, surveillance, ops, and what they were told by confidential informants. We're told Crime Stopper tips were also helpful in the development of the case.

"In what authorities say is one of the biggest drug busts in Milwaukee County's history, police say Phillups' distribution ring was responsible for putting at least seventy-five kilograms of heroin on the streets of Milwaukee each month. The U.S. attorney for the Eastern District of Wisconsin says thirty-five suspects are in federal custody as of this morning, and there will be many more on the indictment. I'm Jessica Mathis reporting live, for IMJ 4. Back to you, Tony."

"You're free. Just take a deep breath. Breathe!" I told myself, as I'd awakened on the plane in a cold sweat.

I'd dreamed that I was still incarcerated. That day, I was sitting at a table in the dayroom playing Spades wearing an orange jumpsuit, when the indictment rolled down on me like an avalanche.

Though the scene continues to roll through my mind, it was over. I landed in Vegas two hours ago. It was my day, and with all that was going on back at the crib right now, I thought it would be a good time for me to come out here and unwind.

Doe actually insisted on my escape. Renting a Jaguar, I'd just been cruising around for a while. Passing the Luxor, it looked so good to me I decided to stop and get me a room. I'd seen and dated quite a few women since I'd been home. But my heart was in search of that perfect match. That diamond. Someone solid, that would make me a better man. I hadn't found that shine I saw in Intimate so many years in another woman. I was beginning to feel like I'd never find love again.

Then, by fate or chance I spotted her. As I walked in the Lux she was coming out of one of its many restaurants. She was beautiful. About five-six, a hundred and twenty-five pounds, wearing a watermelon silk blouse, jeans and heels that matched her shirt. The way her body swayed with her swagger.

The confidence in her stride told me everything without speaking words. Her nut-brownish skin complexion was flawless. I had one chance to get it right. Otherwise, I may never see her again. She could be from anywhere on the planet. I couldn't let this moment pass me by.

"Excuse me, I've got a question." I stopped her as she headed toward the exit.

"How can I help you?" The scent of her perfume was sending me on a continent high.

"What's your name, beautiful?" I asked.

"Athelia," she replied with a smile, giving me her hand. "And you are?"

"I'm Teague. May I ask where you're from?"

"I'm from right here in Vegas. Why?" She laughed. "I'm assuming you're not?"

I said, "I'm not. And I know we don't know each other, but I find you very attractive. I take it you've already had lunch?"

"Yes, I have," she replied.

"Well, it's actually my birthday. I'm wondering if you'd be so kind in joining me for dinner tonight. I hate eating alone."

"Uh, I don't know—" She hesitated. "Where did you say you're from?"

"Oh, Milwaukee. Milwaukee, Wisconsin."

"Okay, Mr. Milwaukee, where were you planning on eating tonight?" she asked.

"The choice is yours. I'm just a visitor. This is your city."

"Well, are you staying here at the Luxor?"

"I'm hoping to. I don't have reservations since the trip was a spur of the moment decision. I was actually just coming in to grab a suite when I noticed your beauty."

She said, "Dinner, I'll have to think about. I can help you get that suite though. I work here. Follow me."

K'ajji

PART II

THE WELCOMING

K'ajji

CHAPTER 23
Hood

I was at the crib laid up when Lue called screaming that Cyn's water broke, and they'd rushed her to the hospital. I told her I was on my way. I couldn't believe she was really about to have this baby. I jumped in my Blazer, turned up the bangs and got in traffic. Me and Money actually pulled in the parking lot at the same time. He'd gotten out and started walking. I ran right past his ass. Seeing the Lacs, the Camaro and the Beemer out there I knew my girls were already in the building.

The receptionist at the front desk told me Cyn was on the second floor in room 205. When I got off the elevator, I ran into Bri, Mu, and Sweets in the waiting area.

"How is she?" I asked, rushing in.

Mula said, "She's still in labor. Lue and her mom and dad up there with her."

The other elevator dinged, and Money came strolling off. He was wearing all black, and enough gold to put Mr. T to shame.

"What up, y'all?" He smiled.

Sweets yelled, "Nurse, here go the father right here! What the fuck you mean, what up? We been waitin' on yo' slow ass. Nigga, they're about to give her an epidural! You better get in there."

At that very moment, we heard Cyn let out a scream to the heavens.

Everybody looked at each other.

"What you say they doin'?" Money asked.

I said, "An epidural. It's a shot to reduce the pain. They shoot it in the lower back. If she moves during the procedure, she can be paralyzed for life."

He looked as if he was about to pass out.

Though I didn't like this nigga for my girl, I wrapped my arm inside his like we were about to get married. "Come on. I'm goin' in there with you."

The nurse escorted us in to see about my sis.

K'ajji

A few hours later, Cyn finally had the baby. It had been weeks since Money's return to Racine from his so-called trip to the Mil and Chicago. T.G. had taken everything. She'd took all of her and Gee's clothes as well as the furniture. Although he'd called pleading for their return, she wasn't trying to hear it. On top of all that, Cyn was pissed at him too. Liquor became his cushion.

Something in my girl's heart had her hooked on this nigga. He was back in Milwaukee, and for the first couple hours of him being there Cyn acted like she didn't give a fuck about all that T.G. had revealed to her. She'd made it her business to call and brag about how Money was on his knees outside her mother's house the day before. I knew that shit had to hurt. Cyn acted as if it hadn't fazed her one bit, and she was still his down-ass-bitch no matter what. It was either that, or she didn't give a fuck. She hid it well. Deep down, she was burning up.

Money had no idea how close to death he'd actually come.

CHAPTER 24
Money and Cynthia

Three Weeks Later....

I'd just came back from making a move with Kilo in Chicago. When I entered the apartment me and Cyn shared, I smelled food. The mellow sounds of *Keith Sweat's Make It Last Forever* flowed from the stereo. I stashed the two duffel bags full of bricks in the hallway closet and headed toward the bedroom.

I opened the door to find the room empty. Sherrice wasn't in her crib, so I figured she had to be in the kitchen with her mommy. I couldn't wait to see her. I threw my jacket across the bed and followed my nose.

Entering the kitchen, I saw Hood and Brianna sittin' at the kitchen table cutting tomatoes and shredding cheese. Cyn stood over the stove lookin' sexy as ever. She was barefooted, in a T-shirt and Capris. When Bri and Hood saw me, I paused, putting my index finger to my lips shushing them as I crept behind Cyn wrapping my arms around her waist.

At first, she thought I was Hood playin'. She threw an elbow.

"Hood! Uh-uh, girl stop!" She laughed. She saw the rings on my fingers. Laying her head back on my chest, she smiled. "Oh, hey, Papi. You hungry?" I smooched her lips.

"You know I am. Where my other baby at?"

"She at my momma's," she replied, still cooking. Her thinking I was Hood had me thinking.

I said, "Tasha, what the hell you been trying to do to my woman?" It was a trivial question that I'd asked with a laugh, not half expecting the answer I got in return.

She said, "Shit, everything yo' ass ain't here to do. Now what?" Hood rolled her neck, and she wasn't smiling.

"Wha—what the fuck? You serious!" I was dumfounded.

"Umm-hmm! As a heart attack." She smirked, eyes beaming.

"Money, I am strictly dickly. You ain't gotta worry about Hood. Now how many tacos you want?" Cyn interjected.

I was having a hard time taking my eyes off Hood's devilish, but sexy grin.

"Four, but I'm about to take a shower first," I replied, still staring at Hood. All this time, I'd never known she was bisexual.

"A'ight, go-head." Cyn slapped me on my ass, bringing me out of my trance.

I looked at Cyn then back at Hood. Then back at her again. Hood tilted her head slightly with her eyebrows raised.

"Boy! Don't let her fuck with your head. Gon' take your shower. Your plate will be ready when you get out."

The ladies laughed.

"A'ight," I said, leaving the kitchen. I turned back, "Is you gon' be alright?"

"Boy!" Cyn put her hands on her hips.

"A'ight, I'm gone."

As I left out, I glanced at Hood, she winked at me and smiled.

CYN

As soon as he got out of earshot, Hood's smile immediately turned into a mug.

She said, "You should let me throw that lil radio y'all keep in the bathroom in the shower with his no-good ass."

Bri and I laughed, but she wasn't joking.

"Hell, accidents happen all the time." Hood looked at me, still shredding the sharp cheddar cheese.

I said, "When I called y'all, I swear I had every intention on touchin' him, but I changed my mind. I can't just kill my daughter's father. I mean, it's different. I love him."

Bri said, "Yeah, and his ass lucky. Cause Tre-Tre 'nem was ready!"

Hood said, "Shit, so was my old ladies."

"Shhhh! Y'all stop now! It's off! Let's just forget I asked y'all blood thirsty asses to come in on this one, a'ight? Damn, let's just eat."

Hood smacked her lips but agreed.

"A'ight," she said. "I'll call the rest of the crew back over. I'm glad they made it outta here with all that plastic we had sprawled out and taped up."

"Bitch, what if he woulda came while all that shit was still down?" Bri questioned.

"I don't know how I would've explained that one," I replied putting the cheese in the refrigerator.

"I guess you could've said we was about to paint!" Bri laughed, clapping her hands.

"Bri, shut up, hoe. You ain't funny. But I guess. Maybe."

They laughed.

K'ajji

CHAPTER 25
Money

It wasn't until later on that night and all her friends were gone. Cyn confronted on me on all my shit. We argued, then had make up sex. It was so good we'd gone three rounds and was now working on our fourth to the mellow sounds of Barry, Al B, James and Chico as they belted out the lyrics to *The Secret Garden*.

"What's wrong?" she asked, rolling over on top of me drenched in sweat.

"No-nothin'. I just nutted again."

"Me too," she cooed, grinding her pelvis against mine. She was so wet her juices were flowing down my thighs. "We ain't done yet, though. Let me see it. Come on," she whispered. "Let me get it up again."

"Shit!" I shuddered, as she took me in her hand and gently stroked it.

"Baby, I need a—"

"Put it back in."

"Move, I got it." She took control. As she held it and rode the head I began to rise. "That's right. Get this pussy," she purred.

"Ooh! It feels so good. Keep it right there. "

"Ssssss! Damn, babe." I guided her hips breathing heavily.

Her sweet moans and juiciness had me back at full attention. We went at it for another forty-five minutes before we'd both busted again.

Laying on our backs, we gasped for air. That's when she brought it to me.

"Money, you-you think you're the only one wi-with secrets?" she panted.

"What you talkin' about?" I questioned.

"There's a lot of things you don't know about me. Things I think you should know before you find out the hard way. Let me tell you a little about who you fuckin' with. Then I want you to choose me or her. I don't wanna have to fuck you up. It wasn't supposed to be like this. But now I'm in love with you. I'd really hate to lose you. I fell for you hard, Papi Chulo." She sat up and wrapped the sheet around her body. She was dead serious and crying.

"Wha—what up, baby?"

She said, "Nigga, I'm about to go there with you. I hope you can handle it."

Money

I took a swig of the Hen-dog as I reminisced and weighed my options. These were two of the realest and baddest bitches I'd ever met. Just cause I said bitches, don't get it fucked up. I love both of my queens. What Cyn revealed to me is still heavy on my mind. As she went back, she laughed at times and cried during others. You'll be amazed by what she said. It sure fucked me up.

CHAPTER 26
Cyn

We had our names changed so our past wouldn't follow us here. You know me as Joe'Cynthia Cyn Forntezz. But my real boricua name is Joel-Cynthia Miel Fuentez. I was born to my mother and father, Joseph, and Maria Miel Fuentez of Puerto Rico. Although my parents worked hard to get us outta the slums of the island, we often fell on hard times. Since I was the oldest of two siblings, my little brother was often my responsibility. We were taught at an early age to cherish family, so we're very close knit.

I'm a spitting image of my mother in her younger days. I developed early, and it caused a lot of unwanted attention. It made me very uncomfortable to hear men old enough to be my father whistle and say perverted things, not knowing or caring that I was only twelve and thirteen at the time. As I was leaving the store one afternoon, my beauty and angelic smile caught the attention of a local drug lord and human trafficker.

His name was Hector Cruz, better known as Hex to the slums. As soon as he laid eyes on me, his sick mind declared me as his own. He'd stop at nothing to have his young princess. He made a U-turn after passing me and rode at a snail pace following me every step of the way home.

He'd immediately placed two of his organizations most notorious body snatchers outside our home to monitor the movement of the occupants inside. In two weeks, the men working for him knew all our schedules as if they were their own. It was a quiet morning in May, when Hex ordered his men to take action. They were to take me by any means necessary. Even if it meant the mass murder of my entire family. It was their M.O. Hex and his team had done this multiple times all over the world.

However, they preferred to handle things as quietly as possible. My routine was the same every morning. I'd get up, get Carlos up, then head for the shower. After my hygiene was taken care of, I got dressed and headed down to the kitchen for breakfast. By 7:30, I'd kiss everybody and head out the door for school. Who'd ever think a trip to the store would change my life forever. I was just going for milk and eggs. You know?

Outside in a brown construction van, just a few feet from my home sat Hex's men. As I walked toward the van, an eerie feeling came over me. The man in the driver seat looked as if he wanted to eat me alive. I never stood a chance, not realizing what was yet to come. As soon as I crossed the rear taillight, two huge men exited the van's back doors wearing ski mask, pointing their weapons.

They'd moved so swiftly; I didn't have a chance to scream. One snatched my legs from under me, while the other covered my nose and mouth with a white cloth. It was the last thing I remembered seeing. When I awoke, I found myself handcuffed to a bed. My vision was blurred, and I had a big headache. I looked around the room in a frightening manner, not knowing where I was. There wasn't much light in the room.

I could smell fresh paint. My eyes searched for a phone, a TV, a clock. Anything a normal room would have. A window, but there were none. I saw a lamp sitting on a table. Next to it, in the far corner looked to be a chair. Looking closer, I took notice that I wasn't alone. Someone was sitting in that chair. Sitting there, staring was Hex.

He switched the light on and stood up. Standing about 5'7, he was bald with craters in his face. He was dressed in an all-white tux and a red tie. I was terrified, bound, spread eagle, and duct tape covered her mouth. I tugged and jerked at my chains, but there was no use. A single tear rolled down my face.

As he stood up and began to move closer, he spoke, "The Chloroform should wear all the way off soon. Right now, you're feeling drained and dizzy. Maybe a headache. Awww, don't cry, my sweet." *He wiped my tears.* "I know you're scared, but there's no need to be. I'm not going to hurt you. Okay."

"Emmmph! Em! Em!" *I was trying to speak.*

"Okay, okay. You want to say something? I'm going to remove the tape, but if you scream, I'll get angry. Now, we don't want that, do we? Hold still. This may be a bit painful." *He snatched the tape off my mouth.*

"Ahhhh!" I moaned, turning my face from him. The sting shot to my nose. "Who are you?" I asked, my voice shaken with fear.
"My name is Hex. And you my dear, belong to me now."
"Wha-what! What do you want?"
"I want for nothing. I have what I want. You're here, aren't you?"
"My family doesn't have money," I pleaded.
"Money? This isn't about money, sweetheart. You're special to me, and I want to make you happy. Rosa!" he called out.
A lady entered the room. She was Hispanic, overweight and homely. "Yes, Senior?" she replied.
"Get her some food. Feed her, then I want you to very carefully cut the clothes from her body." He looked at me. "Don't you worry. I have new ones for you. You'll love them."
My eyes lit up in horror. I closed my eyes in an attempt to wake up from this nightmare. Unfortunately, this was no dream. Hex left the room. Rosa uncuffed my feet and one of my arms from the bedpost. I was able to sit up.
"I be right back with food," Rosa said in broken English. When she got to the door, she turned back. "Do not try escape. It's pointless. No one ever does." She left the room.
My vision started to clear up. I was able to observe the white walls and high ceiling of the room I was being held in.
There wasn't much besides the King-size bed I was chained to. The wooden floors were hard and shiny. There was another door in the room.
Perhaps a closet, I thought. A bathroom, or my way out.
I yanked and pulled at my chained wrists using what little strength I had in my legs. The bed post was built into the wall and didn't budge. I'd pulled so hard I almost broke my wrist. The table, chair and lamp that sat in the far corner looked heavy and expensive. If I could manage to break free one of the three would have to do as a weapon. I pulled the chains once more. The pain was excruciating.
"I see youu!" A voice startled me. It was very loud.

83

K'ajji

I looked around the room but there was nobody there. Searching my surroundings to see where the voice could've possibly come from, I saw a tiny speaker and a camera mounted to the wall. I was under surveillance. "Relax, my sweet. You're home! I'm going to make you feel goood! Relax," *it was Hex.*

"You sick fuck! Aaaahhh!" *I screamed in frustration, I heard nothing in return but silence. No one heard me.* "Help! Help me! Somebody!" *No one answered.*

Since there were no windows, I couldn't tell if it was night or day. Getting down on my knees, I prayed for strength, "He who dwells in a secret place shall abide under the shadow of The Almighty. I will say of The Lord is my refuge and fortress, my God in Him I will trust."

It was my favorite passage. Psalms 91. As I prayed, Rosa reentered the room wheeling a silver cart. On the cart were sandwiches, fruit and juice.

"Why did you bring me here?" *I questioned my captor.*

"I not allowed to answer questions, young one. Only to warn you of certain consequences of not doing what you are told."

"You're not going to get away with this! My dad will—"

"You dad will die trying to find you!" *Rosa tried to break any spirit of hope I had. Her words had hurt me so badly I was speechless. She ordered me to eat as she left the room again.*

Though I was both, hungry and thirsty I couldn't eat or drink anything. It was hard for me to think straight. I was in a state of fear, depression and anxiety. I was restless trying to figure out how, or when I'd see my loved ones again. Some time had passed before Rosa came back pushing a second cart. It looked the same, but there was no food on this one. This cart held all kinds of cutting utensils. Scalpels, scissors and knives.

At the bottom were all sorts of lubricants and sex toys. I was in for a long night. In Rosa's pocket, I saw the butt of a gun. Seeing the handle, I immediately began to sob.

"What is thaaat?" *I cried out.*

Rosa pulled the gun from her pocket.

"Recuff your other leg!" *she ordered.*

The Streets Will Never Close 3

Being scared, I did what I was told.
Seeing I was hysterical Rosa set the gun down on the cart.
"Shhhhh! I have to get you undressed, Cynthia."
"But why! Why are you people doing this to me!" I cried.
"Hex loves beautiful lady. You are his prize, you'll bring pleasure and a lot of money. Now be very still, kay." She grabbed the scalpel, and in one motion she'd cut the colorful buttons up the middle of my silk shirt exposing my bra. My cries grew louder as Rosa slit the middle of my brassiere. My breasts were now bare. Rosa then grabbed the scissors and began cutting my jeans off starting at her left ankle.
"Stop! Please stop! Nooo!" I screamed. I squirmed, kicked and twisted her body. There was no way she'd get my pants off with the fight I was putting up. I wanted to keep my virginity.
"Okay, we do it hard way. You'll get it anyway! May as well be now." Rosa stepped back to the cart and grabbed the pack of syringes. She opened them and abstracted 4ccs of a brownish substance from a vial she'd pulled from the white lab coat she was wearing. It was Heroin. "This will help us both get through this. Hold still, or it may hurt, and it doesn't have to." She grabbed my foot and snatched off my sock.
She injected the potent narcotic between my toes. I drifted off to another place. I still heard, felt and saw what was going on.
There was suddenly this feeling that was new to me. I felt too good to fight. Rosa sliced off my pants and my panties, grabbed the shredded garments and threw them in the trash. I was completely naked. Hex entered the room. He was wearing one of his custommade white towel robes with his name stitched across the back in bold red letters. He excused Rosa as he walked over to me. He ran his finger along my naked frame admiring my young figure. He took a gulp of his Cognac, then set the glass down on the cart next to his tools. Reaching in his pocket, he grabbed the handcuff key then let his robe drop to the floor.
I was repeatedly raped and drugged throughout the night and wee hours of the morning. When my high finally came down a day later I found myself chained back to the bed. I wanted to ball up and

die. *My body ached all over from what he'd done to me. However, it wouldn't be the last time. This was simply the beginning. The rapes continued, as well as the drugging. Soon days turned into weeks. Weeks turned into months. He'd shot me up with so much heroin, I'd quickly became addicted and dependent of it. The only way I would eat, was if he'd promise me more dope.*

As I told Money my story, we cried together.

He said, "Damn, Cyn! He raped you?" he asked. "Why you ain't—"

"Money, just listen. There's more. A lot more. Just listen."

"A'ight."

'But what if I tell you too much and you don't—"

"You won't. Keep goin."

"Okay."

CHAPTER 27
THE SWEETEST JOY

Hex had his way with me hundreds of times over the months and was now losing interest in me as his little playmate. He no longer had me chain to the bed to keep me from trying to escape.
I was never sober enough to conduct any sort of plan. He'd now started sending clients in to have sex with me at $10,000 per head. He'd even made small talk about selling me at one of his underground auctions. He was sure he'd receive a healthy price for who'd he'd called his Puerto Rican Beauty. For two years, authorities searched for me. Our family feared the worse but there was always hope that I was still alive. TV profiler, John Walsh had even done a segment of the case on his hit show America's Most Wanted. He'd taken my case personally, being he too had lost a son to kidnap and murder.

Carlos was now twelve. His young heart was hardened by the fact someone had taken a person that was so special from his family. They'd taken his sister and his family's happiness. No matter how rough things had ever gotten, we'd always had each other.

There was now a missing piece. Our mother cried herself to sleep every night and Pops was devastated, blaming himself for not protecting his little angel. Police were going off the statistics that said most children that are taken, don't survive the first forty-eight hours. Carlos put everything into working for Kilo. It was his way of easing his mind of the pain he felt missing me. He was still in school though.

Kilo made sure the grind didn't interfere with his education. He was moving weight faster and more consistently which impressed his mentor. The impression Carlos presented was hunger. This meant a lot to Kilo. It reminded him of himself when he was Carlos' age. One night, Carlos received a call from Kilo. In his mind, he found this was unusual being he'd always knew specific times the boss would be calling.

Never had they parted without him saying, "Wait for my call. I'll call you on this day, at this time."

K'ajji

When Kilo told him, he needed to see him, and to meet him at their spot in La Perla Carlos was somewhat nervous. The cliff dives with missing limbs were no longer just a rumor that floated around in his mind. He'd been there to witness the horrors for himself. Kilo knew exactly when the sharks liked to feed and boy, did he love feeding them.

One particular time, he shot a guy his hands, his ass and his feet. He tied his hands behind his back, then gave him a choice.

He said, "You know what, I'll let you live. But if I do, I'll go get your mother, your wife and those two pretty little girls of yours. They'll take your place four a.m. tomorrow. So, choose." He smiled. "You jump, or they jump. Same bullets in the same places. What you wanna do?"

He jumped. It was like the sharks were waiting on that ass too. As soon as he hit the water, they attacked him, taking pieces from him at a time. It was almost like they were playing with him, as they circled and came back for him after taking an arm or a leg. Like they'd seen his ass up on that cliff with an ultimatum. The only thing that eased Carlos' mind, was that it was only 11:30 p.m. It wasn't quite feeding time. He'd just made a drop for over four million dollars. He was sure all the money was accounted for.

He and Lamone had counted every penny themselves. If somebody had fucked up, it surely wasn't them. When he said it was urgent, he knew it had to be very important. When he got to the spot, he saw Kilo dressed in all-black and smoking a Cuban cigar. He was leaning against his 1975 black and yellow Chevy Laguna. Resting on his shoulder was his favorite weapon an AK-47.

Carlos' mind was racing, *AK, all-black and a cigar? Somebody was about to die.*

"What up? All the money was there, right?"

Kilo smirked. "Of course, always. Check it out. I have good news for you, Papa' but you're dressed all wrong."

He shook his head. "What do you mean?" Carlos looked down at his attire. "I'm dressed fine. Where we going to one of your clubs or something?"

"Hell nall. Pussy is good, no doubt. But, besides money and chocha, what's better?" Kilo asked.

Carlos had no idea as he thought on it. "Dinero? Chocha?" he questioned.

"Fuck it. What's just as sweet?" he asked.

"I don't know." Carlos shook his head.

"Come on! You know this. I taught you this. Don't think so much on the question. Just look at the man that's asking you. Now, what's the sweetest joy next to gettin' pussy?"

"Revenge?" Carlos replied, dubious about his answer.

"Emm-hmm!" Kilo took a pull from his cigar and blew a cloud of smoke into the air. "Ha-haaa! That's my boy!"

"But revenge against who?" Carlos asked.

"What I mean is this." He took another hit. "Your sister." His voice strained, he blew out the smoke. "She—she's alive. I know who has her."

Carlos' eyes beamed with excitement. He couldn't believe his ears. "Wha-what!" He ran his fingers through his hair, then over his face. "Where is she! How did you?"

"Come on, Carlos. I'm Kilo." He shrugged.

"But how?"

"Well, how I found her is, she's still on the island. My uh, my cousin. How should I put this? My cousin was doing some clubbing when he saw her. That's how I found out this piece of shit Hex has her."

"*A club?*" Carlos looked at him. "She wouldn't. Is she—"

"No, she wouldn't. Look, Hex is a man that runs a little dope here and there. Compared to us, he's smalltime. He makes his living off prostitution and human trafficking. He kidnaps girls from all over the planet. He has never been stupid or reckless enough to snatch one here in Puerto Rico because this is his home. That's until Cynthia. Most of the drugs he moves are within his operation."

"So, what are you saying?" His eyes teared up.

"He keeps his women strung out on cocaine and heroin as a leash, Papa." Kilo held his gaze. "Yes, he has her using. My cousin said she doesn't look all that different, but she was definitely high.

K'ajji

He would've snatched her last night, but Hex's security was too tight."

Carlos paced back and forth.

"Don't worry," Kilo said. "I have eyes on her as we speak. The next question is a stupid one, but I gotta ask. Are you ready to go get her?"

"More than ever," Carlos replied, wiping his tears of anger.

"I had a feeling you'd say that." Kilo smiled, tossing his cigar. "Check this out. Come on take a peek."

They took the few steps further rear of the Laguna. Kilo popped the trunk. Inside, was a small arsenal of handguns, along with masks and a few black jumpsuits. A florescent light illuminated at all. Macs, 9s, .45s, .38s, HKs and .38Os. All the weapons were of different sizes. Carlos selected two nine millimeters. Our father owned one, so he knew a little about them.

"That's it?" Kilo asked. "That's all you want?"

"Yeah, I want these." He looked over the steel. "Grab a mask, some gloves and one of those jumpers to throw on over your clothes."

Carlos was ready within seconds. He'd even thrown on the ski mask before Kilo closed the trunk.

"Now, I have to explain this to you before you go on this mission with me. I've placed teams at a few clubs that Hex owns here on the island. Once I give the order, those teams are going to murder every employee Hex has working for him. Men and women alike. This is the catch. Only the women he has working for him as slaves will be spared. Even pedestrians will be executed."

"But how will they know the difference?"

"Hex makes sure all his staff are dressed in all white from head to toe. All his slaves wear red lingerie. He's been around a long time. His favorite colors are red and white. Tonight, those same colors he uses to demonstrate his power, will be the same colors that sees to his demise. You with me?"

"Let's roll!"

"My boy." Kilo smiled. "Oh, yeah, one more thing."

"What's that?"

"I'll let you kill him."

They jumped in the car. Carlos laid his seat as far back as it would go. This way, no one would see him fully masked. This would be his first time killing someone. He was ready to kill as many people as it took in order to get his sister back. His mind raced in every direction as they rode in complete silence.

He gripped his weapons.

"You know how to use those right?" Kilo looked over at him.

"Yeah. Pops takes me out all the time." He cocked both weapons.

"And me and Lamone sneak and go shoot on our own sometimes too."

The Laguna was roaring powerfully with speed. Within twenty minutes or so they'd arrived at one of the clubs Hex owned. This particular one was called Expectations. There were a lot of expensive cars and trucks parked outside in the lot. They could hear the music's bass thumping through the club's walls. One armed guard stood next to the greeter out front. They were both dressed in all white tuxedos.

"So, this is it?" Carlos asked, as he peeped the scene from low in his seat.

Kilo didn't even speak. He just sucked his teeth like there was a piece of food stuck in them and nodded.

"Well, let's do it." Carlos raised up in the seat.

"Hold up a minute." Kilo held up one finger. He picked up his walkie-talkie and gave the order using one word. "Quell!"

The two men at the door were instantly sniped. From the shadows, Kilo's men emerged like some sort of phantoms. They flooded the entrance at least a hundred deep. Carlos and Kilo watched and listened as the music was quickly replaced by loud screams. Gunfire lit the club up inside as if someone was playing with the light switch. Thirty seconds later, Kilo's walkie came to life.

"Teams one through six, all clear."

He said, "Okay, now, we go in." Kilo pulled his mask down and grabbed his K from the back seat. He and Carlos got out, and calmly strolled into the club guns in hand.

K'ajji

When they entered, there were bodies sprawled everywhere. Blood, brains and guts were splattered from the floor to the ceiling. There was silence besides the sounds of a few sniffles and cries that could be heard over the chatter of the walkie-talkies. All the ladies wearing red lingerie were lying face down on the floor.

The man of the hour, dressed in an all-white tux, with a red bow tie emerged. A Mossberg pump rested under his chin. It was the moment of truth. Automatic weapons were pointing at him from every direction. He was sweating badly, seeing all his men were down, and his reign was over.

"Look who was in the office," the delta team's leader said with a laugh, as he led him slowly down each step.

Kilo greeted him. "Oh, Heeeex! You-gotta—lotta-e-splaining to do!" he said, mimicking *Ricky Ricardo* from *I Love Lucy*. "You took my family as one of your personal slaves Hector! You should really be more careful." It made Carlos feel good to hear Kilo referring to me as family.

Hex didn't speak. He had no idea who the men were. They could've been anybody. He'd kidnapped, raped, and sold thousands.

"Where is Cynthia Fuentez!" Carlos yelled.

Kilo was surprised. It was a voice he'd never heard from the young hustler. I stood up. I was among the girls lying on the floor covering their heads. I was high, shocked and scared. All the gunfire and dead bodies had me in a daze. All I knew was I'd heard my name. I trembled with fear. Discombobulated, I didn't know what to expect. There was so much blood.

I'm going to die! I thought.

Kilo said, "Come to me, Cynthia. You're going home!"

"Home," was all I managed to say.

Hesitantly, I walked toward the masked men. One of them wrapped a blanket around me. I was suddenly surrounded and being led out.

Kilo fired his AK into the ceiling of the building.

Lah! Lah! Lah! Lah! Lah! Lak!

"The rest of you girls are free to go! Get out!"

Lah! Lak!

The ladies got up and stampeded toward the exit. They were slipping, falling, running on broken heels and bare footed. They all were half naked, as they ran for their lives. Carlos remained still, chest heaving up and down, his eyes never left Hex's, who was now on his knees humiliated by defeat. He simply dropped his head. Carlos walked over to him and emptied thirty-four rounds into his face, head and chest.

"Closed casket!" He calmly exited the building.

Over a two-week period, Kilo exterminated Hector's entire bloodline. Anyone associated with Hector Hex Cruz was found murdered or had simply disappeared. He wouldn't risk anyone seeking revenge and coming for our family again. He had them all killed, man, woman and child. He'd uprooted and eradicated his family all across the country. His men left his mark by using his signature weapon, AK-47.

K'ajji

CHAPTER 28
BREATHE AGAIN

I was back home. However, we were all so traumatized by what happened, the family decided to leave Puerto Rico. It seemed as though the police who were investigating were clueless as to who'd saved us. I had no idea myself until some years later. My brother couldn't help bragging about being my savior. The few girls the authorities managed to round up mentioned that the masked men were looking for me and had actually asked for me by name. I actually think the police knew Kilo had everything to do with it, but he paid well. It's said that they were happy to be rid of Hex and his crew. Of course, we ended up moving to the Mil's East side. My brother decided to stay when we left the island, but he did come this way to make sure we were straight.

He actually paid for everything, telling my parents it was a gift from Kilo. He hired our family psychiatrist, got me in rehab, got me a good tutor for my home schooling, plus put me through karate so I'd know how to protect myself. He came to Milwaukee three times a year to check on us until some shit went down on the island, and he had to go on the run. He then stayed in touch by phone. I was fifteen. It would be a whole year before I'd be healthy, clean and ready to rejoin society.

My mother and father retired so they could be with me full time. Carlos and Kilo made sure we didn't want for anything. I was ready to start back attending school. I enrolled in Riverside High. I was feeling good being back in school. Being the new girl in town, everybody took notice of me real quick. At sixteen, if I must say so myself, I was super fine. At five-foot four I wore a 36C. I had this same 28-inch waist span with the measuring tape for this ass!

Dudes referred to me as "Beamer!"

Before I started school, Kilo flew me out to New York to go shopping. I hit everything from Macy's to Fifth Avenue Saks. My gear game was officially crazy. What really took the cake, was when I pulled up in the student parking lot at Riverside, my first day in

K'ajji

my brand-new drop top Benz 190. I'm tellin' you, it was like God had hit slow motion on the world's remote control.
I stepped out of the Benz, hair down to the small of my back. My shit has that natural curly wave to it. I wore a white Versace blouse to match the Benz. A black skirt, and black Stilettos. My skin, flawless, smooth and creamy. My diamond necklace and 2 karat diamonds in my ears took it to another level that they weren't used to seeing in the Mil. Every step I took, all eyes were on me and I knew it.
I heard, "Daaaamn!" from the fellas.
"Who's this bitch?" from the ladies.
I just smiled and waved like the true bad bitch I know I am. Competition was no longer new to me. Thanks to Hex, and all the women I'd dealt with throughout those years of bondage I was game to it.
Every step I took, my ass bounced, my thick thighs and titties leaped and shook with every stride—every step!
Boom! Boom! Boom! Boom!
Ooooh! I'm bad and I know it.

***

"Damn, bae, I didn't know you've been through so much."
"Don't judge me."
"I'm not. Never will."
"Yeah, it's fucked up. But it is what it is. It made me who I am today. You haven't heard the half."
"I'm glad yo' brother murdered that bitch. For real. What's up with 2Hood and them though? How you meet them?"
"My bitches." She smiled. "Let me tell you."

CHAPTER 29
WHAT UP, WHAT'S HAPPNIN'!

As I made my way to the main office to get my schedule, I'd caught way too much attention, but I loved it. I had a crowd of dudes following me, and Lucinda Lue Thicke was right there watching it all unfold. The dudes that were following me called themselves, *The Wolf Pack*. They were on me like a fresh piece of meat, giving me their signature growls and howls, when Lue intervened.

"Ow! Ow! Ow! Owwooh," they howled.

"Dang! Y'all give the girl some space!" Lue wrapped her arm in mine and pulled me at a quicker pace.

I just looked back at the boys and smiled flirtatiously as the howls grew louder.

"Owoooh! Ow! Oww! Ow!" they continued.

Lue turned and said, "*Owooh*, my ass niggaz!" She turned to me and said, "Girl, don't mind these fools. They do this crazy ass shit all the time. I'm glad they ain't hiding the fact that they some damn dogs! Runnin' around here barkin' and shit!"

She frowned at them. "I'm Lucinda. They call me Lue. What up? What's happnin'?" She smiled.

"I'm Cynthia. Cynthia Forntezz."

We shook hands and our friendship was born.

"Nice to meet you. I assume you're on your way to the office to get your classes? Am I right?" she asked.

"Yeah, girl," I replied shyly. "Will you show me where it is?"

"Sure, I can be late to homeroom. I'll just ask the principal to have his secretary write me out pass. Wait a minute! Girl, I know you ain't no freshman? I saw you pull up." she said, looking serious as ever.

"Junior," I said, giving her my sad puppy impression, poking out my bottom lip and slanting my eyebrows. I was hoping she wasn't a senior and wanted no parts of me. I needed a friend.

"Heeey! Me too!" She smiled and said, "We may have some classes together."

"I hope so. I think I'm going to like it here," I replied.

"You will! I'll have to introduce you to the girls. Where you from?"

"Puerto Rico."

"Oooh! For real? I bet it's beautiful over there, huh?" She made this face, like she was in awe.

"It's very beautiful, in most parts."

Lue's cream mixed chocolate skin tone was radiant. She had chinky eyes and full lips, standing about 5'5. She wore her hair permed and cut to perfection. Her measurements were 34-26-42, she defined her last name, Thicke! She had that China Ann thing going on. Good personality, funny, sweet and most importantly, real. When she told me that she ran point for the varsity squad at Riverside, we found out we had one more thing in common besides being young and beautiful. A love for basketball.

We grabbed my schedule from the office. The principal, Mr. Morgan gave Lue a pass for the day she wore around her arm. He'd given her permission to see me to all my classes before heading to hers.

"Okay, I see you've got a few classes with me. We got first, third, and sixth hour together. We gon' kick it!" she said, "I know everybody! I hoop, I'ma star." She dribbled through her legs with an invisible ball, spinning and imitating her fade away. "You hoop for real?" she asked.

"Yeah, I do a lil sumthin'-sumthin'. Me and my lil bro use to play a lot when we were little."

"Well, this my third year running point for V-Squad. What up? You wanna tryout?" she asked.

"Girrl, I don't know."

"Come on! All the PYT's on the squad! You'll fit right in. Well, if you can really ball?" She eyed me as we walked the hall.

"Wait. What the hell is a PYT?" I asked.

"Some say, Pretty Young Thang. It's Pussy You Touched to others. Look, we got practice tonight. I'll explain more later, you'll see."

"Girl, you's a fool with it." I smiled.

"I know." She winked at me.

We'd made it to my homeroom. Lue said, "A'ight, you're right here in 319. Ms. Patterson's cool. Just go to your right when you come outta there. I'll meet you in the main hallway, a'ight?"

"Okay, girl," I replied.

"A'ight, see you next hour."

What Money didn't know was that the PYTs wasn't just some group of girls on a basketball team. He'd let the pretty faces and the bangin' bodies fool him. Shit, I can't front. They'd even had me fooled. In the Murda-Mil, these young ladies flew the coop early. They were much more than your average beautiful females in designer clothes. It went much further than just them occasionally trading in their Chanel, Gucci, MGM and Guess for sweats and gym shorts.

These girls were stickup kids, and murderous when it was essential. When Lue introduced me, she'd simply introduced everybody by name and position. The rest of the shit came to light over time. I'm not sure if Money was ready for all that I've got to tell 'em. M—but here we go! Time to fill him in and see what happens.

"You ready to hear the rest, Money?"

"Yeah, go ahead. How you meet the rest?"

"You sure?" I looked at him sideways.

"Girl, stop playin' and finish tellin' me."

"A'ight, listen."

K'ajji

CHAPTER 30
P.Y.T.

The eight-hour school day went with the quickness. It was time for practice. Lue was excited about introducing me to the team. The last bell rang, and we'd met up in the main hallway.

"What up, Cyn? I'm about to introduce you to the squad!" she said as I walked toward the gymnasium.

When we walked in the gym, Coach J had everybody in lay-up lines doing drills.

I was nervous.

Lue yelled, "Yo! Yo! I want y'all to meet Cyn! She gon' tryout!"

Even though I hadn't really decided whether I was gonna tryout, now I was put on the spot.

"Damn, diamonds and shit!" Karm said being sarcastic. "You gon' tryout in Stilettos?"

Everybody laughed.

"Nall, I got her," Lue said. "I got some gear and some shoes I'm sure she can fit. You're about my size. Anyway, this is Karm, Ms. Shotty."

Karma Sweets, A.K.A. Karm, or just plain Sweets to some. She was the shooting guard on and off the court. Her weapon of choice, her sawed off shotgun. She was very protective of her girls.

She said, "Lue, where you find this one? I ain't never seen her before."

Eighteen year old, Karm stood 5'7, she was Mexican and black and very exotic looking. Her banana skin complexion with specks of freckles made her even sexier. She often dyed her long, black hair red to match her skin tone with her thirty-four double D's her body wasn't short stopping. The hooters made up for what lil ass she didn't get from her momma. Having a twenty-four-inch waist, a thirty-six-inch hip span, and a cross like Jewel Loyd! She's good! Red bone!

Lue said, "Shut up, Sweets. This is my girl Pam, also known as The Aggressor."

K'ajji

"Hey, Cyn!" Pam said with a smile as she went up for a finger roll.

Pamula Vick, A.K.A. Mula, cause she's about that cash. She plays small forward with game like Mya Moore, ain't shit a bitch on earth can do to stop her. She wears her hair wrapped in a bun on the court. When she let her shit down, it drops to her ass. Her Native heritage mixed with black, her coffee cream skin tone drove niggaz nuts! She was 5'8 and stacked with a figure that said 36-25-39. A real powerhouse. Weapon of choice, twin 9 Berettas.

I said, "Hey, Pam," sounding all shy and shit.

"And this my girl Bri. The quiet one. Don't let her fool you."

Lue grinned. "Hey, Cyn, you look nice. Love the blouse." Bri greeted me with a smile.

Brianna Bri Hines the team's starting Forward is like Ms. Candise Parker of the game, literally in both worlds. Her looks said quiet, shy, innocent and sweet. In reality she was deadly and dangerous as a game of Russian Roulette. She was Nicki Minaj bad! Brown eyes, butter complexion, long hair, dimples and all. Just gorgeous! She had luscious pillow lips and a beautiful smile to match, the sight of her made niggaz wanna holla, she stood 5'9 and had a body that reads 34-25-41, she was a real heart breaker. On the low, her weapons of choice are twin, .38 Specials.

"Last but not least, this is my girl Tasha. She's the super freaky one. Think fast, Hood!" Lue yelled, tossing her a rebound that bounced in our direction.

"Hey, Cyn, baby. Yeah, I'ma try you. I mean, you tryin' out?"

"Hood, stop playin' so much!" Lue frowned.

The crew exploded with laughter. I didn't catch it.

Tasha 2Hood Phillups is big sis and big homey of the squad, at 5'10, she played Center. Hood's bisexual. She loved dudes but preferred something edible at times. She was built like a horse. No need for the tape. She's got a top like Tocarra and a bottom like Maliah! Imagine that. With hands like a young Laila Ali, dudes don't even bother approaching her about women she'd snatch with her mean head game and oversized dildos.

Hood was both, beauty and beast. Her weapon of choice, Twin, Colt .45s. The girls were skeptical about my game, until they actually saw me in action. My game spoke for itself. I got heart. I'd managed to score a triple-double on Lue their first scrimmage. Coach J and the others were very impressed. I'd made the team as the number-two point guard.

***

"A'ight now, bitch! I said tryout, not show out!" Lue yelled, giving me a shove.

The locker room grew silent. I just looked at her, wondering if she was serious. I sure looked like she was. We were nose-to-nose staring at each other.

Somebody behind Lue yelled, "Cyn! Cyn! Cyn!"

The rest of the team joined in on the chant started by none other than Karm.

"Don't make me fuck you hoes up!" Lue couldn't hold back her smile any longer.

We laughed until their stomachs hurt.

I had unknowingly passed my first test. I'd made the team.

CHAPTER 31
SHOT CLOCK

The PYTs had been friends since early childhood. Their mothers were close, pushing strollers around the hood together so they'd been riding a long time. When Michael Jackson dropped Thriller in 1983 and they heard P.Y.T. they swore up and down, he was referring to them specifically. The name became official. They were playing in the State Semifinals against their longtime rivals and defending champions, Washington High. There was only zero-point-five seconds left on the clock, Bri went to the rack for a layup.

Washington's Shooting Guard, and star Katrina Tree Young fouled her so hard, she was ejected from the game. The foul caused both teams to leave their benches, and a scuffle ensued. After the refs got everything under control and Tree out of the gym, Bri lined up for her free throws. The gym was so silent, you could hear a pin drop. She sunk the first shot. The crowd went crazy with cheers. At a tied game, she was still holding her form like Jordan, but with one hand on her hip. The ref blew his whistle and gave her the ball for her second attempt. Again, there was silence. As she dribbled the ball, she decided to taunt the other team.

Some called it cocky. She called it confidence.

"Y'all see that! See that shit? Tryin' to hurt a Pretty Young Thang!" She spun the ball in her palms, put her legs into the V shot for the lead.

Everybody paused as the ball left her fingertip, rotating slowly as it glided toward the goal.

Swoosh! All net!

The crowd went bananas! The game wasn't over though. It was still Riverside's ball with 0.2 seconds left.

"D-up! D-up!" the coach from Washington yelled.

Mula handled the inbound pass. She threw the ball to Lue, being that she was the fastest on the team. Lue caught it and ran in circles. The buzzer sounded. The Lady Tigers beat the longtime champs by one.

K'ajji

Karm started yelling, "PYT! PYT! PYT!" Every student, parent, teacher and fan of Riverside joined in as Washington's fans filed out the building. It's been PYT ever since.

CHAPTER 32
GOOD GIRL GONE BAD

Six months had passed, and I was spending more and more time with the crew. Me and Lue were the closest at heart being we'd met first. Thinking back, I often wonder where I'd be if she'd hadn't come to my rescue my first day at Riverside. I gleamed at the fact I have such good friends. They treated me like family, but I wasn't officially PYT. Though I was with them on a daily, they'd never let me kick it with them on what they sometimes referred to as, *Girls Night Out* or *Nights on the Town*.

There were nights that it seemed as though they'd left the face of the earth. I'd call their homes or stop by and none of them would be there. I'd go to all of their favorite spots, but they were nowhere to be found. This often made me feel insecure and left out. I had a strange feeling the girls weren't telling me something. My intuitions were on point.

Every few months or so, they'd get these shirts made with some sort of catchy phrase on them. It was something to let muthafuckas know that they were one. The majority of the shirts they had made were red and black, though they had a few that were pink and white as well. It was time for my second test, and they knew exactly how to bring it to me.

They needed to grab everything they'd needed to put their plan in motion. Since school let out at 2:15 p.m., it gave them a little more than two hours to hit the Grand Avenue Mall, get back to Bri's, shower, dress and wait for me. Everybody was ready. They knew I'd pull up no later than 4:45 p.m. It was our daily ritual. The plan was to grab matching fits and act like they were going skating at The Palace without mentioning or inviting me. They'd took turns peeking out of the curtains to be sure their plan worked to pure perfection. At 4:40 p.m., I hit Sherman Boulevard. Lue spotted me.

"Everybody chill! She just pulled up!" she screamed excitedly.

"Turn the music up!" Bri yelled, as the girls scattered into position.

K'ajji

Mula ran in the bathroom. Bri grabbed the phone off the wall in the kitchen and was acting like she was talking to a nigga. Sweets and Hood were in the full-length mirrors in the living room, acting like they were putting their finishing touches on their hair and makeup. When I got out of the Benz, I couldn't do nothing but smile. I could hear Brianna's momma's stereo all the way up at full blast. It was a clear indication that Ms. Hines wasn't home. I could also hear some of them trying their best to sound like stars as they sung along with the music, and their voices screeched like crows.

Now you say the juice is sour/It used to be so sweet
And I can't help but to wonder/If you're talkin' 'bout me
We don't talk the way we used to talk/It's hurting so deep
I've got my pride I will not cry/But it's making me weeak
I'm not your Superwoman/I'm not the kind of girl
That you can let down/And think that everything's okay
Boy I am only human

It was Karyn White's greatest hit to date, *Superwoman*. Hard to believe she was only eighteen when she'd recorded that shit. Anyway, I knew the girls loved the song. I'd seen them wearing T-shirts with, *I'm Not Your Superwoman* written across the back. Shit, I'd also grown to love the anthem.

I knocked on the door.

"Hey, girrl!" Lue greeted with open arms, embracing me in a strong, sisterly hug.

"What up, Lue-Lue!" I said as I squeezed and rocked her from side to side.

I came in, and took off the black suede jacket I was wearing. I had on zebra skin pants that showed off my curves, a black halter top and white Stilettos. I paid no attention to the fact that Lue had changed since I'd seen her last at school. Until I started looking around. Mula pranced out of the bath-room like she was modeling for Tyra Banks! Bri was in a deep conversation with Tone, Dial Tone. Sweets and Hood were still in the mirrors singing, acting as if they hadn't noticed my arrival. When I waltzed over to the stereo and pressed pause on the tape deck, that got everybody's attention.

108

I said, "Aw, hell naw! You bitches is cold busted! Tell me why all y'all got on matchin' red T's, black GUESS and the new Flight Air Jordan's and ain't nobody told me shit!"

I turned toward Lue, hands on my hips, forehead tensed, mouth hung open and face on gas!

"Oh! Now, you see a bitch!" Lue said, emphasizing her words with her hands.

She walked toward me, throwing her hips and smiling as she spun around. My feelings were hurt, but I tried to play it cool. Crossing my arms, I twisted my lips to the side.

"Where y'all goin'?" I asked with a hint of attitude. "You hoes be disappearing and shit! I finally caught y'all asses!"

Hood said, "The Palace. Ain't nobody tell you?"

I looked at the crew and they were all silent.

"Hell naw!" I said. "Don't nobody ever tell me shit! Ugh, y'all make me sick! Let me see, bitches!" I flopped down on the couch, pouting.

Looking at the shirts, I'd heard the song a trillion times over the past two weeks. Now, one of its main lines were Stretched across the crew's chest. I read the words out loud.

"Yo, what happened to peace?" I took a deep breath and exhaled. "Turn around! Let me see the back, hoes!" I demanded.

As the crew gathered around Lue, they all turned around to let me read the back of their shirts. Going down the back diagonally, all their shirts read, *Peace!*

Peace!
   Peace!
      Peace!
         Peace!

It was homage to Eric B. & Rakim's album "Paid In Full". It was also a hidden statement toward their secret status quo. P.Y.T. was on their right sleeves, nicknames on their left.

"Ooooh, y'all, that shit is fresh! I want onnnne!" I said in my kiddy voice. "I ain't goin' like this, and y'all ain't leaving me!" I protested, poking my bottom lip out giving my sad puppy impression.

They knew I'd react in this manner. Simply out of love for the fly shit.

"Where y'all get the fits from?" I asked.

Karm said, "Come on, Cyn. You know our spot. The Grand, baby."

Lue said, "You know—ya know!" She gave Mula a high five.

"Now, you can have all this and go with us—but there's a catch," Bri said, spinning around, showing off how her black GUESS hugged her ass and thighs. The tiny Jay's on her feet went perfectly with the fit.

"What's the catch, Brianna?" I asked.

Hood said, "You can't buy nothin' but the shoes, baby."

"Wait. There are a few other things she can buy." Lue rose her hand, while clutching my shoulder. "The letters, and an extra pair of shoe strings!"

They all busted out laughing.

I was confused. "What y'all mean I can't buy the stuff?"

Hood said, "Shit, we know you got the money to go buy all this shit and some. That's easy."

"We wanna see if you got enough heart to go take what you want, like we did," Lue explained.

At first, I thought they were just bullshitting me. That's until I no longer saw smiles.

"Y'all serious?" I asked in disbelief. Lue gave me a nod. "Y'all macked that shit?" My eyes were buck wide.

"Yup. The pants, shirts, earrings and all," Mula stated proudly. "I never get caught. Shit, we've learned from the best. My auntie Keba can boost anything. Check it out. We already got the bags from old purchases made from every store you can think of. All the bags are lined with aluminum foil. The metal detectors never go off," Hood broke it down to me.

Sweets said, "So, you still on some *I want shit?* Or are you ready to go take some shit?"

I said, "Fuck it! Where the bags?" Bri walked over to the closet. She went in and came back out hoisting them up. I said, "Y'all rollin' with me, right?"

Lue said, "Of course. We gone."

***

The ladies are thick as thieves, literally. Capitol Court and the Grand Avenue Mall were their favorite places to hit. Everywhere we went, we were the center of attention. That day was no different. There was a group of dudes shadowing our every move as we journeyed from floor to floor.

"Hey, y'all see these dudes following us everywhere we go?" I asked the crew, looking over my shoulder.

Mula said, "Girl, we been peeped them upstairs at the food court. I gave the short one a wink and smile. They've been on us ever since."

"They're kinda cute." Lue looked back and smiled, as we boarded the escalators.

"Yo! What happened to Peace!" one of the dudes yelled.

We all giggled.

One of the others said, "Peace! Peace! Peace! Peace! Peace!"

It was crazy, because as if we were all thinking the same thing, we all turned to 'em and chucked the deuces. The smiles from us musta sparked the confidence they needed to approach, instead of following us like some groupies. We took pause from what we were on for a minute to converse with the group of four. While I was rushing Bri and Mula, I'd accidentally exposed the fact that we were in the mall stealing.

"Will you heifers hurry up! I still gotta mack me some jeans!" I was thinking about my GUESS.

Hell, I'd said it like it was an everyday thing. No shame at all. The dudes seemed genuinely shocked. They found it amusing that such beautiful young ladies could actually be stealing. I guess we looked innocent enough. Anyway, with that being said, we said our goodbyes and were off to get the rest of my outfit. I'd passed that test with flying colors. Not even breaking a sweat. By 9:30 p.m., we were all at The Palace, skating the night away.

K'ajji

CHAPTER 33
THE PALACE

The entire rink erupted when the D.J. spun one of the most infamous skating records ever made. The bass of the song's intro set it off! Then, the aliens spoke, *"Rock—rock planet rock/ Don't stop—"* Everybody sang along with the lyrics of the song. *Jam on it/Jam on it/I said jam-ja-ja/Jam on it.*
Everybody that was somebody was in the place to be. Repping for the ladies, you had, The Knockout Queens, 2-4 Bankettes, The Taylor Clique, Conney Crew, The Sahara Gang, America Posse and last but not least P.Y.T.! As far as dudes, you had, The 2-4's, Hillside, Parklawn, Westlawn, North Ave, Clark, Capitol, Burleigh and Hampton. As always, The Knockout Kings were too cool to put on skates, they were in their sneakers ready to start some shit. Members of the Bankhead family were in the building as well. Male and female. Can't forget 2-7.

Being that it was one of Hip-Hop's greatest years, the trends and the music hit the Midwest with tremendous force as it did the rest of the world. Niggaz were draped in dookey ropes and sweatsuits. Everything was on display from Reebok, Nike, Adidas, Puma and Troop. Three and four finger rings covered their hands. Kangos were worn as if they were some sort of crown. All the Dapper Dan's GUCCI and Louis Vuitton leather coats and jumpsuits stomped the scene.

The ladies were wearing the latest styles we'd seen in videos and magazines like, *Word Up.* Chanel, MGM and GUESS. Hell, big Bamboo earrings were everywhere. The hair styles worn by MC's also made a statement. Dudes rocked high top fades in the likes of dudes like Kool G. Rap. While ladies tried their hardest to get their shit whipped like their favorite artist of the year. Things had come a long way since the birth of Hip-Hop in the early 70s. It's said she was born in the 1500 Block of Sedgwick Ave. in the Bronx. It was a house party thrown by, the notorious Kool Herk. Legend has it that it was there that the first record was purposely scratched, giving birth to the queen, Hip-Hop.

K'ajji

Every song the D.J. spun got the rink hyped. He hit 'em with, *It Takes Two* by Rob Base & DJ EZ Rock! Then, he pumped, *No Half Steppin'* by Big Daddy Kane! When he spun *Push It* by Salt-N-Pepa, the ladies went bananas!

Salt and Pepa's here/Salt! Salt! Salt/Salt and Pepa's here! Every female in the building sung along.

"Heyyyyy! This my joint right here!" Lue yelled to me over the loud music.

We'd separated from the crew, putting on our shoes to go grab some pizza and soda for everybody. Little did I know, the PYT's weren't there to just skate and have fun. They were there scoping their next lick.

The dude they'd planned to stick next was a nigga the streets called 2-4 Action. He was a pretty boy ass nigga that was gettin' plenty of money. He fucked with a chick name Zoi from the Sahara Gang. Just like most niggaz gettin' it, he was a hoe and was known to get around on his bitch. This would soon become his downfall. Zoi being one of the baddest chicks in The Sahara Gang, Action had no reason to be cheating. It was just his nature, I guess. Ranking second in command to Sahara herself, Zoi had clout. A lot of niggaz even felt she was colder than Sahara.

They just never got at her out of respect for her dude. Action and Zoi had been together for six years. Rumor had it, they were married. The P.Y.T.'s really didn't have a problem with Sahara or her crew. But to get at Action, causing a scene would likely be their best route. That way, Action would believe he'd be in the clear of being back stabbed if he took the bait, they intended sending his way. The girls had already decided they were going to intentionally start a fight with The Sahara Gang, by sending Bri at Action. Hood, Mula, Bri and Sweets were racing around the track, and it was time to bust a move.

"Bri-Bri!" Hood yelled over the sounds of Push It.

"What uppp!"

"You ready to bust that move! I just seen Action and them 2-4 niggaz hit the floor when we rolled by! Roll down on 'em! We're right behind you!"

The Streets Will Never Close 3

"A'ight, I'm on one!" Bri replied, speeding off.

Bri took off around the rink, spotting her potential vic. She'd also flew past Sahara and her crew as if she hadn't even seen them. She hit her stopper on the front of her left skate as she approached the 2-4 brothaz skating six deep.

Brianna rolled up to Action, without saying a word she swerved in front of him and started grinding her body against his to the beat as Salt and Pep sang the hook.

Ssss-Ahhh/Push it!

Action was enjoying the new found attention from the mysterious beauty. Bri changed the words to the song. Instead of Salt-N-Pepa's, push it good.

She sang, "Pussy Good! Ssss-ahhh! Pussy! This pussy real good!"

The Sahara Gang ain't like that shit at all! Sahara was first to take notice.

"Zoi! Oh, hell nall! Who is that skatin' with yo' man rollin' her ass all up on him like that!"

"Where?" Zoi asked.

"Bitch, you don't see that shit!" She pointed. "Where—

"Right there, bitch!"

Action and Bri were heading toward them. The Sahara gang was six deep, but so were we, being they'd brought me along.

"Okay! Shit's about to jump off! Y'all see 'em right?" Hood asked Mula and Sweets.

"Yeah, we see 'em! And we ready for whatever. I got my razor just in case shit gets out of hand," Mula said with a grin.

Hood said, "It won't. Just stick to the plan. But, if it do, I'm knockin' Sahara out first, then Zoi." The gang was getting closer. Hood said, "Okay, now!"

Hood, Sweets, and Mula sped up to catch up with Action and Bri. The 2-4 brothaz with Action had left him alone to skate with his new friend. My girls and The Gang rolled up on Bri and Action at the same time. The Sahara Gang surrounded Action, catching him by surprise.

115

"Um, excuse me, Action! Nall, fuck that! Eric, who this bitch!" Zoi yelled, trying to grab Bri's arm, but she snatched it away.

They all stopped in the middle of the floor causing a few collisions and falls.

"Hold up! Who you callin' a bitch!" Bri started taking off her earrings in fight mode.

Action just smiled and said nothing. He loved drama.

That's when Hood rolled in. "Bri, what up? You good?" she asked, with Sweets and Mula right by her side.

"Yeah, I'm good! This broad just came at me sideways like she tough or somethin'! Called me a bitch! I guess over this nigga!" Bri crossed her arms and rolled her neck.

"Bitch, do you know who the fuck I am!" Zoi said, trying to get at Bri.

She launched, but Action grabbed her and wrapped his arms around her waist. The commotion gained a lot of attention.

Lue saw the plan in motion, and me and her ran over there to aid and assist our girls. Sahara and her people looked like they wanted to jump something.

"Y'all don't wanna do that! I'm tellin' you now!" Mula warned cuffing the buck-fifty in the palm of her hand between her fingers.

Action said, "Zoi, you trippin'! We was just skatin'!"

"It didn't look like y'all was just skatin' to me! Shit, it looked like y'all was about to fuck right here in front of everybody! You had your greasy ass hands all on her hips and thighs and shit! I seen ya ass, muthafucka! Get off me!" Zoi yelled.

"Yo, chill! You embarrassin' yourself. I don't even know this girl!"

"That's right, hoe, check ya dude. You don't want none of this, but he do. I'll take yo' man!" Bri smiled.

Lue said, "P.Y.T., we lookin' too cute for this shit. We out. Our food should be ready anyway."

"And we want it hot," Bri said, staring at Action seductively.

"Oooh! This bitch think I'm playin'!" Zoi struggled to get free from Action.

The Streets Will Never Close 3

As we were leaving, Bri smacked herself on her ass and rolled her eyes at Zoi.

"Sahara! Timber, get this nigga off me! Why y'all ain't do shit! Them hoes talkin' all reckless and shit!"

"Zoi, your man knew you were up in here! And not taking sides against you, you my bitch! But you need to check his disrespectful ass!" Sahara said, pointing her finger all up in Action's face.

He said, "Sahara, girl you better get your lil ass finger out my muthafuckin' face!" He was still hugging Zoi from behind.

Oleta said, "Let her go, nigga! We got her!"

"Nah, I got her. This mine. Y'all go head. She'll catch up to y'all in a minute." He loosened his grip on Zoi.

Zoi said, "You ain't got shit, nigga! You better go holla at that stank hoe you was just with." She gave him a shove and rolled out with her girls.

"Checkmate is in order. Looks like the king just lost his queen for the night," Bri said, as we watched everything play out from the concession area eating our pizza.

Sweets said, "It look like they're about to bounce. They're changing into their shoes."

"Well, it's either that, or they're coming this way so we can fight. I just saw all of 'em look this way. And ooh-wee! Zoi heated!" Hood laughed.

Lue said, "Wait a minute. Okay, I see 'em. Yup, they're heading toward the door. I guess plans have slightly changed. I'm sure the nigga Action will be over here any minute with his two-foe buddies trying to get the digits."

I was again lost in the conversation. I'd seen Bri skating with dude, but I had no idea who he was, or what Lue meant by plan. I wanted to ask what was really going on but decided against it. I thought maybe it was a plan to take the girl's man or something. Just as Lue predicted, within minutes Action and his friends were at our table as soon as his girl and her crew departed.

"Excuse me, ladies." Action showed a smile. "Excuse me, Ms? I didn't catch your name." He was giving Bri a seductive eye.

117

"You never asked, and I never threw it," she replied with a smile looking him up and down. "It's Bri." She extended her hand to him. He took it inside his and kissed it.

"I'm Act—"

Bri cut him off, "Also known as Eric Charlse."

His homeboys started laughing.

Rockwell his right-hand man found it hilarious. "Damn, dog, she used your gov."

Action was surprised. "Damn, since you already know me, can we take a seat?"

"Nah, we don't know you niggaz like that. Besides, ya lil' girlfriend might come strolling back up in here." Bri flirted with her eyes.

"Damn, it's like that?" Action asked.

"Yeah, for now. You can leave me your number though. I'll give you a call."

"Okay. Okay, I can dig that. But how you know my name though?"

"Boy, duh! When you was going to school, and emphasis on *was*, you was the star receiver at Vincent. You also played Shooting Guard for the varsity squad. One of the best in the country. I do read the paper. I've also seen you play a few times. But since you're a few years older than me, I doubt you would've noticed me back then. I'm shocked you gave all that up for the streets."

"Damn. That's deep. A lot of people act as if that shit never happened when they see me. Anyway, let me go to the counter and write my number down for you. Don't disappear on me, alright."

"I won't," she replied.

He looked at his crew. "What the fuck? Y'all niggaz ain't said shit! By the way ladies, this my man Rock, Alias, Josey and Dookie."

Bri said, "Pardon me. Where are my manners? This is Lue, Cyn, Sweets, Hood and Mula. Say hey, ladies."

"Hey," we replied, with no enthusiasm at all.

His friends looked rough. Action left and returned with his number.

The Streets Will Never Close 3

He handed it to Bri. "Here you go, sexy. Make sure you call me. Maybe some of my friends and your friends can hook up?"

"Okay, I'll give you a call."

"A'ight, fellas. Let's ride. See you later, Bri. Bye, y'all."

"Byyyeee!" we all said in unison as the 2-4 boyz left.

"What kind of name is Dookie!" Lue was loud as ever!

We all busted out laughing.

"Shhhhhh!" Sweets said, "Girl, he looked back. I think they heard you."

Lue said, "So, I don't give a fuuuuck!"

We continued to laugh. As the night went on, we had a ball.

K'ajji

CHAPTER 34
Bri's

Over the next couple of weeks, Bri and Action spoke over the phone on a regular. She even allowed him to take her out to eat and on a few shopping sprees. The plan was coming together as expected. He began opening up to her, telling her all about his operation and how much money he made. He claimed to be making up to fifteen thousand a day, and roughly seventy thousand a week.

This was like good music to the crew's ears.

I wasn't a member of the clique as of yet. But with all this shit about to go down, Lue thought it was the perfect time to present the idea to the rest of the squad. They called an emergency meeting at Bri's to discuss how things were going with the nigga Action. Lue used this opportunity to bring up the possibility of me becoming one of them to the fullest.

I wasn't there though. They'd snuck and had this meeting behind my back.

***

Hood said, "Bri, you got the floor. Go head. Give us the rundown on everything you've peeped on this next sting."

"A'ight, check it, y'all. The shits true as far as everything we've been hearing about the boy Action. I've seen and counted some major paper with this nigga myself, so I know firsthand. The nigga got a spot on Wells that pull in five thousand a night when it's slow. The craziest shit is the nigga spilled all the beans and I ain't even gave him none of this pussy. A lot of niggas pillow talk, but this nigga just got loose lips.

"He loves showing out. He took me on a few shopping sprees, and we spent stacks like they were nothing. We've kicked it so tough I pretty much know the entire layout. He don't do no hustling. He don't do shit but get the work and put it out there. From 7:00 a.m. to 3:00 p.m. he don't do shit but go to his spots and chill. He be on some overseeing the operation type shit. That's just the day shift. From 3:00 p.m. to 7:00 p.m. his homie Dookie runs shit. Then, from 7:00 p.m. to 7:00 a.m., his man Rock is in charge."

"Bri, how much money he let you count?" Mula asked, rubbing her hands together.

"I counted fifty thousand one day I'd went with him to collect from some niggaz on Capitol. That was just my pile. He counted a lot, too! And, oh yeah! Before I forget. Mu, he said his man Dookie trying to get up with you on some double date shit this weekend."

"Girl, I ain't fuckin' with that nigguh! With his ugly ass! You illin'!"

There were a few giggles throughout the living room, but the crew had to remain serious. Their lives would be on the line when it came time to lay these niggaz down. Everybody stared at Mula in silence. She knew without question she'd have to go on this date. Two minds are always better than one.

"All right, I'll do it, but I ain't fuckin' him!" Mula stated with certainty. "If Shorty Shit Stain tries anything, I'ma break his fuckin' fingers!" She poked out her lip like a two-year old.

Hood said, "Okay, that's good. I'm glad you agreed to go with her to observe. You ain't gotta fuck. You know that's your choice. Y'all try to find out everything y'all can on his man Rockwell without asking too many questions. Then, we'll decide which spot we'll hit, if not both."

Sweets said, "Bri, how was security looking when y'all went to the spot?"

"I saw two niggaz standing outside the house. Apparently, they use intercoms. We pulled in the alley, and when Action got out, one of the dudes greeted him. When they walked to the back door, Action pushed what I thought was a doorbell, but them niggaz doin' it different. Somebody asked who it was through a speaker. Action said his name. They're over there running shit like it's legal! The nigga's security was standing outside on the side of the crib, broad day with a big ass SK, or an AK-47 on a belt! He was on some military shit."

"Shit, it ain't nothing we can't handle," Mula said, brandishing her twin 9s. "Nina Simone and Millie Jackson love to sing. Don't cha, ladies?" She smiled.

Lue knew the girls were still skeptical about me, but it was now or never. She thought I was ready, and willing to bet her life on her girl. "That's my bitch!"

"It would be nice to have some extra guns in on this next lick." She put her idea up in the air.

Hood said, "What up? What you sayin'? You think Cyn ready to be all the way down?"

Lue glanced at Mula.

Mu said, "Shit, don't look at me!"

"Hell yeah, my bitch ready! I know she'd be down to ride!" Lue was confident.

Hood looked around the room at everybody. "Okay, let's take a vote. By a show of hands, how many think Cyn's ready for the finale to become one of us?"

Of course Lue's hand was the first one to fly. Sweets' was second, then Bri's. Mula and Hood were left staring at one another.

Mula said, "Fuck it. Looks like were outnumbered three to two."

"Come on, y'all! She ready for this shit! I'm tellin' you!" Lue pleaded.

Reluctantly, Hood and Mula both smiled and raised their arms. As Hood's hand raised, Mula was still holding Millie and Nina.

Raising them to the ceiling she yelled, "Two guns up! Keeper of the flame! That's him over there! Let's do it!"

Bri said, "Girrl, calm yo' ass down! You bet not shoot them damn guns in here! My momma will kill me."

They all laughed.

I had one more obstacle in my way. The crew had already tested my loyalty by saying little shit behind each other's backs to see how I'd react. At first, I wouldn't say shit, but then I started checkin' their asses. I told anybody that had something to say that was negative about a bitch, out of respect not to tell me. I don't do messy. There was no question on whether I'd choose a dude over the crew.

All the girls had lil boyfriends, or friends with benefits, but not me. I'd let dudes call me and take me out. When it came to the goodies wasn't shit happening. Hood began to think I was bi, and that would've been right up her alley. Nope. The final test was underway, and the plot was well put together.

CHAPTER 35
BECOMING

It was a Tuesday night, I was at home trying to finish my homework, when my phone in my room rang. I glanced at the clock. It was 11:38 p.m., I was tired.
"Hello?" I answered the phone half asleep.
Hood was on the other end of the line. She sounded out of breath and panicky. "Cyn, one of Lue's old boyfriends just beat the shit out of her! We coming to get you!" She hung up before I even had a chance to speak.
I was losing my damn mind waiting on them to get there. About ten minutes later, Sweets, Hood, Bri and Mula pulled up in front of the crib in Mula's Astro Van. I was already outside, pacing back and forth.
"Come on! Get in, let's roll!" Hood yelled from the passenger seat.
I ran to the van and the conversion door slid open. I jumped in the back with Bri and Sweets. We pulled off.
My first question was, "Where's Lue!" Not seeing her.
"She's in the hospital," Sweets replied, pulling her shotty from beside her thigh.
That was their cue, everybody started upping their weapons to see how I'd react.
"We 'bout to kill this nigga and whoever with him," Sweets said, caressing the sawed-off shotgun.
Hood said, "Yeah, touch this pussy. You down?"
There was no hesitation. Instantly flashbacks of the abuse Hex inflicted upon me flashed in my mind. Then, Lue's beautiful smile. My friend. My sister!
I said, "Let's ride down. Where he at?" I could tell Hood was shocked but smiling on the inside.
"You know how to use one of these?" Sweets asked, as she handed me a Mac-11. It was a beauty!
"Of course I do, I'm from the island," I replied.

K'ajji

I checked the magazine, then slapped it back in. Then I checked the chamber to see if one was up top, it was.

Hood said, "A'ight, Mula, when you hit Port Washington, keep straight till you hit Keefe then bust a left. I know exactly where this nigga stays and get his pay."

"Here, throw this on real quick," Mula said, tossing me a black hoodie.

I put the hoodie on and drew the strings tight enough to cover my face, but not so tight where I couldn't see.

Mula said, "Okay, I'm about to hit Keefe now."

She hit the lights and bent the corner, pulling to the curb. When she turned and pulled over, we saw two dudes about 80 yards up the block standing in front of a house. It looked as if they were hustling.

Mula yelled, "Everybody get down! There go that pussy ass nigga right there!"

When I pull up on 'em, Bri open the slider.

"Cyn, spray them nigguhs. Make sure you kill 'em both. No witnesses. We'll cover you. Make sure don't nobody come out the houses," Mu directed with precision.

She pulled from the curb, sped up and hit the brakes directly in front of them. As soon as Bri slid the door open, I let the Mac ride.

Tat! Tat! Tat! Tat! Tat! Tat! Tat! Tat! Tat! Tat! Tat! Tat! The dudes hit the ground, but I didn't see blood. So, in a trance, I jumped out of the van and ran up on 'em. I stood over their bodies still pulling the trigger.

Tat! Tat! Tat! Tat! Tat! Tat! Tat! Tat! Tat! Tat!

I looked at the Mac thinking, *What the fuck! How these niggaz still breathin'!*

"Cyn, get in!" I heard somebody yell.

I looked at the crew confused, as the two dudes stared up at me from the pavement.

I continued aiming the gun at them. *They're identical,* I thought to myself.

"Come on, bitch! Let's go!" I recognized Hood's voice bringing me back to reality.

Still confused, I ran and jumped back in the van.

Mula smashed out.

I snapped, "What the fuck was that! This muthafuckin' gun don't even work! They're still alive!" I snatched the hood off my head, throwing the gun on the floor.

"Calm down, baby." Hood said, in a smooth motherly tone. "We had to test you. The Mac was filled with blanks."

"What you mean y'all had to test me!" I was pissed.

"We had to see if you'd kill for the team. If you would, you'd pass." Hood smiled.

"You passed, girl!" Karm gave me a tight hug.

At first, I was kind of hesitant, but I hugged her back. My adrenalin and mixed emotions still had me somewhere else.

"Yup, you passed. Didn't know you had it in you." Mula looked at me through the rearview as she drove. "I'm also ashamed to say I had my doubts."

Bri said, "I believed in you!"

"Hold up! Where the fuck Lue at? Y'all hoes set me up!" I finally smiled. "Of course I'll kill for y'all. We family. We P.Y.T.!"

Hood said, "She at home. We're about to switch cars and go get her now. She trusted in you one hundred percent. And yes, we are. P.Y.T., welcome to the other side. You're now officially one of us."

The crew had already staged the scene. Hood has two brothers I didn't know nothing about since they were never mentioned in my presence. They knew exactly how their sister and her crew got down, and the importance of earning trust. They'd created the monsters the girls had become so they'd agreed to play targets for my initiation. After switching vehicles and going to pick Lue up, we headed to IHOP to celebrate. It was there over pancakes, they broke everything down to me.

They told me how they'd pulled kick doors on niggaz gettin' money, and how they sometimes had to bust their guns in the process. That night was the first time I told any of them about what I'd been through with Hector Cruz. We laughed many days and nights together, but that night all of 'em cried for me. They finally understood why I hadn't had a sexual relationship with anyone. The abuse is well hidden, but I'm far from over it. They had my ass crying.

K'ajji

I hadn't cried in years. I wiped my eyes and told them to dry theirs. We had business to discuss.

I said, "All right, y'all. Let's dry these tears. Let's talk about this next target now that I get it. Let me guess. Action, right?" Bri wiped her tears and smiled. "Yup, Action it is. Let me tell you, we already got it mapped out. Me and Mula gon' let the niggaz take us out. We got a date."

CHAPTER 36
DATE NIGHT

"Mu, you ready! I just called Action and he said they're on their way!" Bri hollered through the bathroom door.

"Give me five more minutes!" Mula yelled.

"Girl, open this door! I done seen everything you got already anyways, shit!"

"Ain't, I'll be out in a second! Dang, chill!"

"You've been in there for an hour and a half! Let me find out you trying to get super-duper for Dookie!"

"Damn, how you know how long I've been in here?"

"Ya mammy told me! Now, come on!"

"Ugh, she talks too much, shoot!"

Bri heard the lock click. Mula came out wearing a short, red, fitted dress that showed off her long, beautiful legs. The spaghetti straps on it gave a full view of her cleavage and her back. She looked gorgeous. The dress looked as if it were tailor made specifically for her, the way it fit her curves.

She had her hair brushed to one side laying over her shoulder. Her radiant skin shined. The diamond earrings she had on seemed to dance as they dangled from her earlobes with red Stilettos and red lipstick on her luscious lips, she was almost ready.

"You ready?" Bri asked, barely giving her space.

"Hold on, bitch, I gotta grab my handbag and my whatchamacallit."

She brushed past Bri with her heels clacking as she hurried toward her room. Bri was right behind her.

"You gettin' supa-dupa! Damn, girl! Here I am in some jeans and shit, and you all did up!"

"Well, you never asked me what I was wearing. Plus, we gotta give these nigguhs the impression that we really feeling them, right?"

She browsed over her dresser until she spotted what she was looking for. Her diamond tennis bracelet, she grabbed it. "Here, put this on for me." She handed it to Bri.

Brianna sucked her teeth. "You all brand-new. I ain't never even seen none of this stuff."

As soon as she connected the clasp, they heard a horn blow outside.

Bri ran to the window and looked out. "It's them! You ready?" Looking in her mirror once more, Mula said, "Yeah, I'm ready. Let's do it." She grabbed her handbag that contained Nina.

***

Outside, Action and Dookie sat in his black Delta '88 sitting on chrome and gold Ds and Royal Seals. They were banging *N.W.A.'s, I Ain't The One*, smoking a dubby.

"What up, A? You think they gon' be down to fuck tonight?" Dookie asked, as he lounged in the passenger seat of the root beer-brown, with a chocolate rag and gold trim big body ride.

Action had his shit domed up with the grill, he inhaled. "I don't know, Dook." He held the smoke, then blew it out.

"Whatever you and her talk about is on y'all. I've kicked it with Bri quite a few times, and I ain't fucked yet. So, don't be surprised if you don't hit tonight. Yo', kill that shit. Here they come." He handed the joint to Dookie.

He put it out and threw it out the window.

Dookie said, "Damn, ole' girl and her friend looking good, A!"

"True-that, true-that. Yo, get in the back, nigga."

"Oh, oh shit. You right." Dookie got out, greeting the ladies as they approached the car. "Hey, ladies. Y'all lookin' just as beautiful tonight." As he opened the back passenger door, he left the front open for Bri.

"Thank you," Mula replied. "You're such a gentleman."

"Unlike somebody I know," Bri said, getting in the front seat. She looked at Action with a frown.

Stunned by the statement, Action said, "He a what?"

He twisted his lips to the side looking back at Mula as she slid in. He knew Dookie had just been getting his ass in the back like he told him to.

"She said I'm a gentleman." Dookie smiled, poking his chest out.

"Nigga, just get cha ass in the car!" Action rubbed his beard. Dookie got in.

"So, where we heading?" Bri asked.

"I was thinking we'd go over to Perkin's and grab somethin' to eat. Then, go to the movies, catch Fatal Attraction or some shit."

"Sounds good to me. What you think, Mu?" She glanced back.

Mula said, 'That's cool. I see y'all got the munchies." She laughed.

Perkin's is a well-known establishment in Milwaukee. Famous for its soul food, stars from all around the world have been there to dine.

"So, how you doin' this afternoon, Ms. Pamula?" Dookie asked.

"It's evening, and I'm doing fine. You?"

"I'm good. I-I'm Dookie. I know we didn't get to properly introduce ourselves at the rink that night. But I swear, I've been thinking about you ever since I saw you."

"Aw, that's so sweet. When you thought about me, what were you thinking? What are you thinking now?"

"Well—" He swallowed hard. "Looking at you right now. In my mind, I'm begging that you'll do me this one favor. I mean, cause you a bad chick."

"But, Dookie, you've just met me. What is it that you want me to do sweetheart?"

"Just tell me this. If you can't promise to do it. Will you at least think about it?"

"Well, that depends on what it is," Mula replied, crossing her legs, she looked at him.

"I want you to put cha pussy on my face and just cough."

"What! Boy, you's a fool!" Mula said full of laughter.

Action and Bri couldn't help but to hear the conversation. They'd busted out laughing as well.

"Please do that for me." He was still pleading while they all died laughing at him. Mula blushed. "Turn my lips into a glazed doughnut." He smiled.

Action said, "Dookie, yo' ass crazy as hell, nigga!"
Ignoring Action, he said, "Can I please be your Dunkin Donut?" He spoke with a straight face. Mula couldn't even look at him without laughing.
He said, "All you gotta do is cough. I'll do the rest."
"This boy is funny! Where you find this nut?" He was serious, yet she was so tickled.
Still laughing as he drove, Action could barely breathe. "Dook, how in the hell you gon' ask that lady to skull fuck you! She just got in the car. We gotta talk. Seriously."
"Man, you see this girl back here?"
"Yeah, I see she lookin' good, but damn, homie!"
Bri turned around in her seat. "Mu-Mu, you a'ight back there?"
"Yeah, I'm all right. I'm hoping he was just playin'. I hope."
Dookie leaned over and ran his finger along her thigh. "I wasn't bullshitin'." He tasted his finger, then mouthed the words so she could read his lips. "Donut!"
Mula laughed, but inside she was disgusted as she thought, *Perkin's is right here in the hood. I ain't gotta be in this car too long with Shitty. I mean, he dresses a'ight, and he don't look that bad. Hell, the dude is funny, and I like that. Too bad I might have to dead his ass.*
Arriving at the restaurant, they were greeted by Mr. Perkin himself. He always greeted his customers with love. After being seated, everybody scanned their menu to see what they wanted.
"Action said, "Y'all order up some shit. Everything on me."
"Oohhh, waiter!" Bri raised her hand.
Perkin's junior came over to take their order.
"I already know what I want. I eat here all the time." Bri began running down her order. "I want some rib tips, a side of Mac-N-Cheese, with yams, corn bread and cabbage. And ooh, can y'all sprinkle a little brown sugar on the yams for me, please?"
"Um-hm. Gotcha. Anybody else ready to order?" Young Perkin asked.
Mula said, "Shoot, her order sounded so good. Let me get the same thing."

"Okay. No problem, sweetie." He wrote a two by Bri's order.

Action said, "I want y'all boneless catfish, with a side of spaghetti and meatballs. I'll take garlic bread. I love the way they sprinkle a lil paprika on their fish. Have y'all tried it?"

"Hell yeah! They fish good as hell!" Dookie replied, extra loud.

Bri and Mula just nodded in agreement that they'd tried it, and it was good. Action shook his head at his friend. He was starting to regret he brought him period.

Dookie said, "Yo', waiter, let me get a shoulder dinner and some fires. I'm good."

"Any drinks?" the waiter asked.

"Ladies, what y'all drinking?" Action asked.

"Pepsi." Bri replied,

"Bring us a pitcher of Pepsi." Action folded his menu.

"Will that be all?"

"Yeah, I think that's it for now." Action searched everybody's eyes. "We good?"

"Yeah, we good," the ladies said in unison.

Mula took it upon herself to spark a conversation with Dookie as they awaited their meals.

"So, Dookie, I see you fresh. Adidas from head to toe, with your jewelry and thangs. You doing it. What is it that you do to afford all that?" She smiled.

"Awe, baby, you ain't heard? We run shit. My man, Action, right here eatin' and he make sure the team eats as well. Dope game, baby. We gettin' mon-nayy!" he yelled, raising his arms like he was the king of the world.

He caused everybody in the restaurant to look in their direction.

He said, "By the way, A, I went to the spot on Capitol. Rock said to tell you to come pick that lil hundred-geez up tomorrow around two, or just send me."

"Cool." Action waved him off, as he whispered in Bri's ear.

Jackpot! Mula thought. *This nigga just don't know! He made my pussy tingle at the sound of a hundred thousand!*

"Damn. Y'all doin' it like that? Where yo' woman at? I know you gotta one, if not a few," Mu stroked his ego even further.

He said, "Nah, I ain't got no main chick."

Mula said, "You ain't gotta lie, nigga. You probably fuck with one of them hoes from the Sahara gang. Don't front." She smiled Overhearing the conversation.

Bri said, "Speaking gang-gang, I hear you and Ms. Zoi just had a baby about six months ago." She rolled her eyes at Action while he was trying to woo his way into her panties.

"Is that true?" she questioned.

Action was caught off guard and hesitant with his response.

"Yeah, yeah. That's what's up. I just, we just had a little boy. Uh, where you hear that at?" His demeanor had suddenly changed. Now he was serious.

"Damn, relax, killa. Let's just say I do my homework."

His face showed he wasn't satisfied with Bri's answer.

"Nah, for real. Who told you that?" he asked.

Bri said, "I'm just playin'." She folded her hands. "I was at the shop getting my hair done. You know how shit go at the salon. Gossip!"

Their food had arrived just in time.

CHAPTER 37
WE RIGHT HERE

Outside two blocks away, me, Lue, Hood and Sweets were ducked off in the van. We parked so we could see every car coming and leaving Perkin's lot. An hour and forty-five minutes went by. We finally spotted Action's Delta pulling out of the parking lot. The plan was to follow his ass all night until he eventually went home, which we did, after going to the movies, he dropped Bri and Mula off at Brianna's. He dropped Dookie off on Wells.

We then tailed him out to his crib out on Deer Run Drive. We knew it was where he laid his head, because out in the driveway was his and Zoi's matching Beamers. We watched from a distant as he strolled in the crib. It was like, he hadn't a care in the world.

Lue said, "Got that ass now, nigga. Y'all see this nigga out here in suburbia? Thinkin' mufuckas wouldn't find his ass."

"Pussy you touched," Hood said, taking a pull of the joint, blowing the smoke out her nose.

We pulled off slowly, eyeing the condo carefully as we drove by.

When we got back to Bri's and heard talk of the hundred thousand that was supposed to be picked up the next day, we decided right then and there, it was time to hit Action.

"We goin' in tonight, y'all ready?" Hood asked, searching our faces. "Lue?" she began her roll call.

"Hell yeah."
"Mula?"
"More than ever," Mu replied.
"Cyn, you ready?"
"I'm down."
"Sweets?"
"You already know."
"Bri?"
"Cheah!"

K'ajji

Hood said, "A'ight, y'all know the drill. Show Cyn how to wrap up. Give her the rundown while I go grab the tools from the crib. I'll be right back." She hit the door.

I said, "*Wrap up?* What does she mean wrap up?"

Lue said, "You, well, we all have to put on these sports bras, then wrap our chest with ace bandages. That way, when we go in, they won't know we're females. The oversized jeans, masks, gloves and hoodies will hide the rest. This is the blueprint on how we usually do it. Hood has the deepest voice. She can sound like a nigga at will. She's the only one that speaks to our captors. So, if you ever hear a word, even a peep from anybody else things are about to go another direction, which means, we're about to gun shit down. You understand?"

I said, "Understood. Say for instance, one of us is in danger and we have to expose ourselves. We shoot first and ask questions later. Hood's voice is the only one I should hear, right?"

Sweets said, "Right. Because once we're in, we duct tape every bodies, everything. Hands, feet and most importantly their mouths. We make sure every room is secure, then Hood does her thing."

Mula said, "We already got some extra gear for you. And, since you handled Lue's Mac so well during your audition-- "

"I'ma let you hold down one of my babies for the night," Lue interjected. "You'll have fifty rounds of the real thing tonight girl. But we don't kill unless we have to. Okay? But this will only be temporary you know? You holding down Maxine in all."

"Uh, okay, I guess."

"I ain't playin'! Take good care of her now."

"I got her." I smiled.

As we wrapped each other's heads and breasts, the crew was calm. They'd been through it several times before. Hood came back through the door ten minutes later carrying a huge duffel bag.

She sat it down and unzipped it. "A'ight, y'all. Choose your weapons of choice, as always. I snatched up some new shits from Spencer's through a friend of a friend. That way shit can't be linked back to us worst case scenario. This time we're goin' in as Gremlins! Check it out, I got gear, too. All black everything."

136

Sweets picked up a few masks, looked at them and said, "Damn, girl, all these ugly ass masks. They ain't have no Gizmo masks or nothing besides these?"

Hood said, "Shit, we ain't trying to be cute. I told him to grab something intimidating. Remember how shook niggaz was when we wore them Freddy Kruger masks? I think these are perfect." She pulled one over her head, covering her face. "See, *Raahhh muthafuckas!*" she'd barked loud like a dude and I jumped!

Everybody else laughed.

Lue said, "Ooh! You show is ugly." Like Shug told Celie on The Color Purple.

We all laughed.

"All right, now!" Mula said, interrupting the laughter. "We gotta get to this nigga's crib! Let's get this shit on. My palms got an itch."

Sweets said, "She's right, time is money."

Hood took off her shirt, exposing her bra. "Somebody, wrap me up real quick."

Lue said, "I gotcha, sis."

K'ajji

CHAPTER 38
WHERE THE BAG AT!

The clock in the van read 2:20 a.m. We were posted outside Action and Zoi's crib.

Lue came and jumped back in the van, out of breath. "I-I've been around the-the whole house. There's only one light on, and that's in the bathroom. There's a glare from the TV in the living room. I couldn't see if there was anybody on the couch or not. Other than that, there's no movement. We've got the front door, the patio doors and the inside door that leads to the garage, of course. Two floors, maybe a basement, plus a back door. No alarms, no security lights and no dogs, which means—"

"We go in quiet." Hood took over from there. "Okay, Sweets. We need you to jimmy the locks to the front door, so you're in with me. Lue and Cyn, cover the patio doors until we let y'all in. Mula and Bri, that leaves the back door. Once we let Lue and Cyn in with the Macs, we'll cover them, and they'll open the back door for y'all. Now, if there's anybody in the living room on the couch, me and Sweets gon' handle that before we do anything. If not, we'll sweep the house together as one broom. A'ight, everybody ready?" We all nodded. "We ready. Let's touch 'em then."

Everybody exited the van, spreading out and falling in position. Sweets sat her Shotty down on the ground, while Hood had one of her guns trained on the door and the other on the windows in front of the condo. Within seconds, both locks were picked.

Sweets whispered, "We're in." She tucked in the lock picks, and grabbed her Shotty.

She turned the knob gently and cracked the door. Hood pushed it open moving swiftly, .45's up. Sweets covered her as they moved in silence. Hood moved quickly toward the living room's couch, while Sweets pointed her weapon at a closed door, then a staircase leading to the second floor. Hood cleared the living room holding up two fingers. She signaled, they checked to see what was behind

139

door number one, by pointing two fingers into her eyes, then back at the door.

Sweets nodded her head and acknowledgment, back-to-back, they move toward the door. Hood pushed the door open. It was an office, no one was inside. She tapped Sweets on her shoulder and threw up two fingers for clear, then nodded toward the kitchen. After clearing the kitchen, Sweets opened the patio door for Lue and I. Sweets and Hood checked the two-car garage while me and Lue let Bri and Mula in the back door.

No basement. The first floor was clear. The team quickly moved up the steps to the second floor. The upstairs bathroom light was on, but it was empty. Down the hall, squeaks and moans could be heard. We paused. Every single gun was now pointed in one direction. The bedroom.

"Oooh!"

Squeak!

"Ooh, shit! Right there, baby."

Squeak! Squeak! Squeak! Squeak!

"Ahh, ahhh. Oooh shit. Not too—Not too hard, Eric, you gon' wake the baby uuup. Ooooh!"

Action continued to stroke with his eyes closed as he hit Zoi from the back. They were so into the sex that they hadn't even noticed the six other people in the room. That's until Zoi open her eyes and found herself staring down multiple gun barrels held by masked intruders. She attempted to warn Action with a scream, but at the first sound of her voice, Hood slapped her across her head with one of her .45s, knocking her unconscious.

When Action heard the steel connect with her head and opened his eyes, his nightmare began. "Zoi, oh shit! What the—What the fuck?" He saw the situation and raised his hands.

Hood took charge. "Shut the fuck up, pussy, before I kill your ass! That bitch a'ight!"

Zoi was out cold, ass still in the air.

"Take your dick outta her slowly and lay yo' bitch, ass flat on your stomach with your arms spread straight out. Keep your hands where I can see them, cause you accidentally go under a pillow for anything! You, ya bitch, or that baby over in the crib won't make it to see another sun."

Action did as he was told.

She said, "Now put cha hands behind your back." He did that as well.

Mula tucked her guns at her waist and grabbed the duct tape and rope from her book bag. She tied Action's hands tight, and duct tape his mouth. She did the same to Zoi while she was still unconscious.

"Wake the hoe up. We going downstairs to the office to handle this business. One of y'all grab the baby. If that little motherfucker wakes up and starts crying, duct tape his mouth, too."

Those are the words Zoi heard as she regained consciousness. When she came to, she was terrified. This wasn't something happening in her sleep. She was bound and gagged. Her home had indeed been invaded. The first thing she saw to her left was Action being led out of the bedroom ass naked at gunpoint. She immediately turned her head to the right to see a dark figure leaning over the baby's crib. She tried to plead, but the duct tape had her lip seals. Tears ran down her face mixed with the blood that gushed from her head. When she saw her son in the arms of one of the masked intruders, her cries grew louder.

Hood ordered her to shut up, get up and walk. "Can't nobody hear what you're saying right now, bitch. But there may be a time where you need to say something. Save that shit till then. We just here for the money and the dope. Now get up and come on!"

When we got them downstairs, we forced Action and Zoi to their knees in front of the sofa. We stood around them in a circle with guns in their face. Hood stepped forward and snatched the tape from Action's mouth. His anger got the best of him.

He snapped, "You niggas is dead! You motherfuckers done ran up in my shit! Gotcha hands on my motherfucking son and my—"

The loud outburst woke lil Eric up, and he started crying. Zoi's eyes bucked at the sound of her baby's cries. She could barely breathe knowing what was next to come. Hood put her .45s to both of Action's jaws cuttin' his lil speech short.

"Now look what the fuck you done did! You done fucked up. Yo', duct tape that lil' muthafucka's mouth and sit his lil' ass right here between mommy and daddy." Mula did just that. "Now, we done killed that noise, let's get down to business! Where the money and the dope at, nigga! We got all mornin'—don't make me torture yo' ass."

Action said, "I got five thousand upstairs in my pants pocket. I ain't got no dope."

"*Five thousand*, nigga, you think I'm playing with you don't chu!" Hood snatched lil' Eric up off the floor by one arm like he was a rag doll.

"Nigga, I swear-to-God, I'll throw this lil' motherfucker in the oven! Where the money and the dope at!"

Zoi's muffled cries and squirm to get free wars were of no use. Seeing the way her baby was being handled was killin' her. Knowing a mother's love is like no other, Hood decided to see if she would talk. Zoi's feelings were so torn, it was hard for her to say anything without her nerves jerking her entire body and soul which made it sound as if she was stuttering.

Zoi said, "He, he got, a-at-at-at least ta-ta-two-two, two hundred thou-thou-thousand up-up-upstairs in our-our bedroom cl-cl-closet in-in shoe-shoe boxes."

Hood signaled me and Lue to go check it out. she said, "Get that five out this fuck nigga's pants pocket, too!"

"Th-th -the dope is at-at-at the spot. On cap-cap-Capitol wit-with Rock. I-I can get it for-for you ri-rig-right now." Zoi nodded her head tryin' to convince Hood.

"Bitch, how are you going to get the dope?" Hood acted unsure of Zoi's offer.

"I-I-I makes mo-moves for Ac-Action all the time. I can go-go grab the-the bricks, I swear! Jus-just pro-promise me, you, you—won't hurt—my-my baby," Zoi said as tears flooded from her eyes.

Hood still had Lil Eric dangling by one arm and she pondered on the idea. Then she thought, *Nall, that ain't going to work. She bleedin' and shit.*

The Streets Will Never Close 3

She was too distraught. She'd come to a conclusion. She dropped Lil Eric on the floor in front of his mama.

She said, "Nall, good look, but—" She pushed Action's head to the side with one of the foe-femps. "This bitch right here gon' make it happen for us. Ain't cha, bitch? Look, this is what you're going to do. Get on the phone, call your man Dookie. You going to tell him you just got word that the police are supposed to be hitting the spot over on Capitol.

"So, you want him to go get all the dope, and all the money off Cap, and bring it to you. Now, if you say anything! I mean anything else! It's hammers. And I'm gon' broil that little motherfucker before I kill you, just cause I said I would. I might fry his ass and save some time! Now, I ain't askin' twice so what's it gon' be, nigga! Bullets and a cooked baby, or you gon' pay me?"

Action said, "A'ight, I'll make—I'll make the call, just be cool a'ight! Damn!"

Action called Dookie and gave him the spiel. Thirty minutes passed before Dookie showed up carrying a red duffel bag. As soon as he extended his arm to ring the doorbell, the door swung open and he was drugged inside. The door slammed shut behind him as he landed on the floor.

"Whoa-Whoa! What the!" Dookie said as he looked up at two oversized hooded Gremlins.

One held a Mac, and one held a sawed-off shotgun. Both were aimed at him. We didn't have to say a word, it was obvious what it was. Dookie looked over to see Action and Zoi, butt ass naked and hogtied, along with four more Gremlins with guns.

Hood greeted him, "Welcome to the party, Shitty! Grab the bag, frisk 'em and come lay his ass down."

"Damn, A, I should have known something was up," Dookie said, shaking his head, hands against the wall as me and Sweets patted him down.

I kneeled, opened the bag and gave Hood and the crew thumbs up to its contents. We shoved Dookie into the living room, hogtied and duct tape his ass as well. Hood clapped her hands. The unique

143

percussive sound of the leather coming together was our signal to move out.

Hood said, "Oh, before I go—don't worry. I'm gon' have somebody call in a domestic dispute at this address. The police will find you within the hour. Wouldn't want the baby to starve to death, now, would we? We all got to eat. Never have so few owed so many!" Were her last words.

***

"It was a line a stick-up kid used in a movie called-- " Cyn began, before Money cut in.

"Uptown Saturday Night, starring Bill Cosby, and Sydney Poiter. It was one of my pop's favorites. Ha-ha ha! Y'all crazy!"

"Hood said she always wanted to use that line. You wanna hear more?"

"Yeah, go ahead," said Money.

"PYT, us never part!"

CHAPTER 39
MAKIIDADA

Back at Bri's, we counted the money we'd taken from Action. After hours of counting, we were a little more than $300,000 richer. That wasn't even including the dope. There were also five bricks of grade A cocaine in our possession. I was in awe.

"Damn! Look at all this money! Woo!" I threw a stack in the air.

Lue said, "So, Rookie, how does it feel?"

Hood said, "Yeah, being your first mission in all?"

I said, "Shit, it feels good! The power! You know what I'm saying?"

"Um-hmm! We know exactly what you mean!" Lue replied dishing out daps to the crew.

Hood said, "It's like busting a nut! Shit, multiple nuts. Y'all, I know you can die from that shit?" We all laughed. She said, "What y'all laughing at? I'm for real!"

Bri startled us. "Oh-oh-oh, shit!" She pointed toward the TV. "Turn it up! We made the news!"

Sweets hit the volume.

We all tuned into the news reporter.

"Good morning, this is Jessica Mathis reporting live from the scene. Just behind me is where a mother and her infant of six months were injured. Police say they were called by an anonymous source concerning a domestic dispute here at the home. Officers say, upon their arrival just minutes ago here at the home on Deer Run Drive, the shocking discovery was made.

"Inside the home, police found its occupants bound with duct tape and rope, in what appears to be a case of armed robbery. Witnesses say a group of six armed men invaded the home at approximately 3 a.m. this morning demanding money from homeowners Zoi Love, Eric Charles, and family friend Darnell Scott who slept on the family sofa. Police are investigating, but there are no suspects. I'm

Jessica Matthews, and this is Channel 6 Action News. Back to you, Jimmer."

"That was Action News a'ight! Ha-Haa! That motherfucker wasn't on no damn couch, was he, Sweets?" Hood laughed.

"Sure, in the hell wasn't! That nigga went from the door- to the floor! *Blam!*" Sweet replied, giving Hood a high five.

Bri said, "Look, we got to split this money up and get y'all out of here before my mama gets home."

Hood said, "A'ight, check it out. It's already in stacks of a thousand, with a few extra stacks on the side. Bri, you and Mula can split those odd few. Everybody grab fifty gees a piece. I'm going to sell the bricks to my brothers for no less than a hundred thousand more. We can bust that down later. I surely don't want to be here when Ms. Hines get here. So, forty-eight, forty-nine." She stuffed her money inside her duffel bag. "Fifty, me and my money and these two old ladies." She referred to her .45s. "We are about to bounce." She zipped up her two duffle bags, picked them up and headed for the door. "Good job, y'all! Ms. Hines needs to work the third shift more often. P.Y.T. I'm out!"

"Me too, y'all." Mula stood up and stretched after bagging her fifty-plus.

I said, "I'll drop Sweets and Lue off. We out, a'ight, Bri?"

"All right, y'all,"Bri replied.

Exiting, Hood yelled, "P.Y.T. us-never-part!"

"Makiidada!" The crew sang in unison.

"Even if they stopped my heart!" Hood echoed, leading the lullaby.

"Makiidada!" I joined in.

We shared smiles, as everybody quickly hit it out $50,000 richer.

"Ain't no mountain, ain't no sea."

Money

"Hold on, Cyn. Y'all should've killed that nigga. I know I would have. That's a lot of paper."

The Streets Will Never Close 3

"Tu no sabes cuantas gana yo tenra de matarta a ti," she mumbled in Spanish.

She does that from time to time. Mainly, when she gets mad. "Now, you know I don't understand that shit. What the hell you just say?"

"Oh, nothing, Money. I just said you just don't know how much I love you. *While you having babies on the side and shit.* I smiled. *You just don't know how bad I wanted to kill yo' ass,* I was thinking, but I played it off. "There's more. You wanna hear or, no?"

"Yeah, over breakfast though."

"Okay, I'll cook and tell you more."

K'ajji

CHAPTER 40
Rock

Reflecting. . . .

A few weeks had passed, and Action was still pissed. His ears in the streets had failed to come up with a lead on who ran in his shit. As he and his man Rock smoked, they had a brief conversation on the matter.

"What's on your mind, G?" I asked, as Action daydreamed.

"Nothing," he replied dryly.

"Yo, you lying, bro. Come on, I've been knowin' you since we was pee-wees, nigga. What up? I see you over there in deep thought."

"A'ight, I'm going to holler at you about that shit. Ain't no since in me holding it in. I told you and the crew that little money and the dope niggas got wasn't shit that could hurt us, and it wasn't. I still can't shake the fact that they put they hands on my motherfuckin' son. Ooh!" He slammed his fist against his coffee table so hard, the legs under it gave away like toothpicks.

He stood up and paced back and forth across the living room.

He said, "Refresh my memory, my man. You said when they came out, you seen 'em jump in a black minivan, right?"

"Yeah," I replied. "I saw 'em come out. I thought they were some of our workers making a drop or pick up like me and Dookie was doing. I ain't think nothing of the black hoodies and shit, until I peeped the mask one of them had on that happened to glance in my direction. You know how you always have us park a little-ways down the street? They parked the same way, but just on the opposite side of the street. They moved at a normal pace but when I saw the last one backing out clutching two burners and wearing a mask, I knew what was up."

I dropped my head in thought. He sat down across from me. Lounging in a brown soft leather armchair, Action thought about all his enemies and who he possibly could have beef with.

"You say you followed them North but lost them in traffic on the highway, right?" he asked.

"Yeah, my nigga. I followed them North on 27th but I lost them. I ain't have no heat with me or you know I would have tried to fill some heads. I was trying to follow them at a safe distance so they wouldn't notice a nigga on they ass."

"Fuuuccckkk!" he yelled in frustration. "All these ears we got to the streets! You ain't heard nothing?" I sighed.

"Nah, man, I mean, it ain't nothing I heard or been hearing. Niggas comparing this shit to all the other niggas that's been robbed over the years. Remember last year, the nigga Tre Rida and a few of his guys got laid down by five niggas wearing Freddy masks, right?"

"Yeah, I remember," Action replied back. "Prior to that, five motherfuckas wearing jumpsuits and hockey masks ran up in Burleigh Rick shit."

"Um-hmm, got 'em for a pretty penny, too," I reminded him.

"Right, the niggas stung him for like two-hundred thousand and ten of them thangs," Action replied.

"There you go, it's a long shot, but I spoke to some niggas from over the way since this shit here has occurred. Do you know ain't none of them niggas ever found out who was behind that shit?" I rubbed my beard in thought.

Action said, "So, you, think it's the same niggas that hit us?"

"I'm thinking it could be, although there was a sixth man. Maybe they just added another nigga to the team. I put a lot of thought into this, my nigga. The only reason I ain't bringing it up to you sooner because I didn't want to come on no halfway assumption types, nah mean? If those goddamn windows weren't tinted, I could have got a good look at them. Whoever the driver was, drove like a pro. They covered that ass. We done snatched up a few niggas that owned black minivans. Did some shit to them that would have made them tell on their mamas. They ain't have shit to do with it. Trust that, I did get wind that a little bitch had a similar van, tinted and all."

"Did you get a name?"

"Nah, I ain't even bit into it yet."

"It definitely wasn't no bitches that ran up in here. But find out who she is anyway and get back at me. It could be her big brother, cousin or some nigga she fucks with. You know what I'm saying?"

"Damn!" I pondered. "You right, I should have thought of that." I took the last, long drag of the joint. Burning my fingertips I put the fire out in an ashtray. As I stood to my feet, blowing out the smoke, I said, "A'ight, homie, I'm about to be out." I showed him some love. "Yo', I haven't been seeing Zoi and the baby the last few times I've been through. Where are they?"

He said, "Man, wifey don't feel safe here no more." He pulled me in for the embrace and we bumped shoulders.

I said, "Shit, I don't blame her."

"Yeah, I moved her and shorty into another crib. We gon' sell this one or go ahead and rent it out."

"Word?" I questioned, eyebrows raised.

"That's word, man, she still shook from this shit. My son's shoulder was dislocated and shit."

"Maaan, I'll see what else I can come up with. I'll be back at you later."

He said, "A'ight, peace, man."

"Until the storm," I replied.

K'ajji

CHAPTER 41
LADIES NIGHT

Over the next couple of months, we were living larger than life. We balled hard! Though everybody stashed a cut of the 300,000 we snagged, when Hood came back with another hundred and ten thousand off the bricks, we went on a shopping spree! Everybody bought new cars, except me. I just added a few accessories to the Benz.

Lue copped a BMW, ironically, it was the same make and model as Zoi and Action's shit, just a different color. Her shit was Royal Blue. Hood bought a red Chevy Blazer that had just come out that year, and Mula copped a black IROC-Z to satisfy her need for speed. Sweets and Bri cool booty asses settled for Lacs. Bri grabbed a Seville, and Sweets went for a Fleetwood. Although all of our gear game stayed official, we copped a gang of shit to go with the wardrobes as well.

When we pulled up to the Red Corvette banging Supersonic by JJ Fad, you couldn't tell us nothing! Niggas was straight jocking our style. Every bitch out there hated witnessing our arrival. Not wanting to show out too much we just brought the Benz and the Beamer out to flex. Ain't nobody know about the other cars in storage. Not yet anyway. When we stepped out of the rides, we were met with catcalls and whistles from every direction. As always, we were dressed to kill.

D.J. Homer Blow went P-Funk for a second banging out *Parliament's, Flashlight* then *Slick Rick's, Bedtime Story.* Every hand in the building was in the air, drinks and all. We were dancing and making a beeline through the crowd heading toward the back.

Hood's older brother Moo-Moo grabbed her by the arm, leaned it in her ear and said, "Leave them I gotta holla at you." He looked serious.

Hood nodded toward the bar, letting us know to go have fun, and she'd catch up. She and her brother headed toward V.I.P where they could have a little more privacy. When they arrived at the table Moo-Moo had preserved, Hood's other brother Doe-Doe was sitting there. He took a deep breath, stood and greeted Hood with a hug, and a kiss on the cheek.

Doe said, "2-Hood, your ass is getting too damn sloppy."

"Have a seat," Moo said sternly, pulling out her chair for her.

Hood took a seat. She had no idea what her brothers were upset about but she knew they weren't for games. Her brother sat down but said nothing and just gave her a mean glare. Slick Rick was still telling his story. The Silence from her brothers was starting to scare her and she didn't scare easily.

She finally broke the ice, "Well, is y'all going to tell me what's on your mind, or just sit here and stare at me all damn night? What's up?" she asked sarcastically. "I know the dope was A-1, so—"

Moo said, "The bricks were good, this ain't about no motherfuckin' work. You haven't heard about all the bodies they've been finding in dumpsters, abandoned buildings, and creeks and shit?"

"Yeah, I've seen the shit on the news. They said some shit about some of them being tortured to death, missing family jewels, hands and shit. What that got to do with me? I ain't cut off— Hold up, wait let me think. Nah, I ain't been cutting off no dick lately." She started smiling.

Doe said, "Sis, this shit ain't funny!"

"Sure, and the fuck ain't!" Moo-Moo leaned in Hood's face as he spoke through clenched teeth so other people in VIP couldn't hear him. He also wanted her to know he meant business. "All these niggas had something in common. The police ain't mention for specific reasons. All the niggas own black minivans, girl!"

Hood's eyes lit up and grew a size bigger as her mind raced.

Doe said, "Yeah, that's right. Just like the one y'all pulled moves in. We've been looking all over for your ass. We had to body a nigga last week cuz word got back that he said something about knowing a broad with a black minivan with tinted windows. Rockwell having niggas hemmed up and murdered trying to figure out who ran in Action's crib. Now, we can't sit back and wait for him to come at your girl Mula."

Moo said, "Which I know you ain't going to do. You ain't having it."

Doe countered, "So, our next option is to bring it to them niggas first."

Moo said, "Ain't no telling if the nigga gave Rock a name or not. Before we murked him, of course the nigga cried like a bitch and swore on Jesus Christ that when he mentioned the shit to Rock, he brushed the shit off without even asking for a name. But niggas will say anything when they're about to die." He took a sip of his Henny on the rocks.

Hood leaned back in her chair and closed her eyes in an attempting to gather her thoughts. *Who could've saw us?* She sighed, then took a deep breath. She held it in for a second before releasing it. Her head hung and shoulder slouched, she sat quietly for about a minute or two. Then, she raised her head. "Look," she said. "I don't think Rockwell and Action got a name or they would have come at Mula already. She and Bri have been in touch, and even alone with Action and another nigga from his crew a few times since the lick. What I'm gon' do is holler at my girls and make sure they haven't missed any tell-tell signs or some funny shit. As far as I know, the niggas just chasing some pussy they'll never get. I definitely appreciate y'all pulling my coat on this shit. We slipped somehow. Do this for me, though. Keep your ears to the ground. See if you can find out exactly who it was that saw the van. Meanwhile, we gon' get rid of the one we been using."

Moo said, "Yeah, y'all do that."

Doe said, "You strapped right now?"

"I keep an old lady with me, she 45."

"Let's get you a drink," Moo said patting her shoulder.

While Hood was in VIP talking to her brothers, we had our eyes on two potential vics in the club throwing money around like it grew in their backyards. We sat at the bar observing the two gentlemen closely as *K.R.S. One's* voice shook the club.

Criminal minded you've been blinded/Lookin' for a style like mine/ They can't find it/ They be the audience/I be the lyricist—"

The two strangers rapped along with the lyrics of the song while flashing wads of money, their jewelry, and designer clothes.

K'ajji

"Ain't nobody gonna move on 'em?" Lue asked the crew. "That's a'ight I got this one. Watch and learn."

She got up and sashayed over toward the two strangers accompanied by four young ladies trying to get some play. Lue boldly walked over and stepped in between them, rudely pushing the ladies aside. Although the song wasn't much to dance to, she moved her hips seductively, stepping to the taller of the two targets. Grinding against him, she then turned her back and bending over to the front, she touched her toes. Her beauty and confidence definitely caught their attention. Though the guys didn't mind, the ladies felt totally disrespected by my young diva.

"Uh-uh! Who's this bitch supposed to be?" One of the females asked the other.

Lue wasn't worried, she continued doing her. When she looked back over her shoulder, she knew she had him. As soon as she felt his hands grasp her waist, she stood back up and faced him.

"Damn, baby, it's like that, huh?" the taller guy asked flashing a smile.

"Yup," she replied with a sexy smile of her own.

She turned to the four ladies that were still standing next to the other dude. "I'm Lue, bitches."

They recognized the young P.Y.T member. They wanted no parts of the squad. Suddenly having a change of heart, they strolled off waving their hands in the air to *Dana Dane's Cindafella.*

"Damn, you're aggressive. Lue, is it?"

"Lue it is, and you are?" she asked.

He said, "I'm Ink, and this in my nigga Serve. Who you wit'?

"My P.Y.Ts." She looked back over her shoulder at us.

Swerve said, "Damn, who is that over there in the black?".

"That's my girl, Sweets. Come on. Let me introduce y'all to my sistas," Lue replied.

CHAPTER 42
INK AND SERVE
Cyn

Moo-Moo was straight chillin' sipping his drink, when he looked up and saw the two strange dudes entertaining us.

"Yo, sis check ya girls out. Who them niggas over there wit 'em?" he asked.

"Them ain't none of Action's people, is it?" Doe clutched his heat.

Hood looked very closely before she answered. She didn't recognize them as being part of Action's team. Downing the last of the five shots the twins bought her, she answered Doe's questions, "Nah, that ain't none of Action's people. Hold up, let me go see what the hell is going on," her voice strained as the Yak burned her chest.

As she stood up to come address us, the Hennessey hit her hard and she stumbled a little bit. It had been a while since she'd had a drink.

"You a'ight?" Moo asked, grabbing her arm.

She said, "Yeah, I'm good. Just a lil tipsy, that's all."

"Damn, that quick?" Doe laughed.

"Shut up, Doe!" she muffed him, scurrying off before he could grab her.

"A'ight! Yo' ass ain't too grown to get beat!" Doe yelled over the sounds of Ready For The World's, *Oh Sheila*.

As Hood approached us, we had our backs to her. I knew she had to hear all the fun we were having with all the laughing and joking goin' on as she got closer. She heard one of the two mention buying out the bar. It was time to end the party as far as she was concerned.

"Who the fuck is you niggas!" Hood roared.

When we turned and looked, there was so much hate in her eyes, I thought if looks could kill, Serve and his boy would've been dead. We were all caught off guard by her demeanor.

Lue tried to calm her down. "Hood, this is—"

"Fuck that!" Hood cut her off mid-sentence. "Bounce, niggas! You niggas gotta be out!" She gave the niggas the thumb toward the exit.

"Damn, wassup witcha girl?" Ink asked.

"These niggas was flashin' heavy. Throwin around that paper, so Lue busted a move," Sweets whispered in Hood's ear.

"Fuck Lue and these niggas! Matter of fact, they ain't gotta leave! We 'bouta to be out!" Hood stated with authority.

"Hood, we just got here. *Fuck, Lue?* What's wrong with you? You're drunk, ain't you?" Sweet questioned catching the slurs in her words.

Hood just stared at her.

"Yup, this bitch drunk. Already." Bri laughed.

"Fuck it, yall. Let's just go." Lue was frustrated.

Hood's last comment had her hot. She didn't appreciate it at all. Before she'd take it there with her sister in public, she'd let it ride. Oh, she was pissed!

"Nice meeting, yall," Lue told Ink and Serve as we headed for the main exits.

When we got to the doors, Hood drew her weapon to her side. "Hold up y'all. Stay close but let me check shit out first."

We saw nothing but a few patrons, some leaving and some arriving. We were unaware of the situation, so I was sure we were all wondering what the hell was Hood's problem? Knowing somebody might've been out to kill us had her on edge.

I said, "Is she trippin' off the liquor, or what?" I thought I'd said it low, but everybody heard me, including Hood.

Looking back at us, she saw the confusion in our faces. She decided she'd address it. "Look, I'll tell y'all what's going on as soon as we get somewhere safe. Bri, is mom home tonight?"

"Yup," Bri replied.

"Damn, Tipp is, too." She racked her brain for another destination for us. "Okay, I got it. We going down to the lakefront for an emergency meeting. But first we gon' stop by the crib and get everybody tooled up. Come on, let's go."

CHAPTER 43
MURDA-MURDA!

We'd made it to our vehicles safely, and left the club, unaware that we were being watched. Rock and one of his goons, G-Dep were lying low in the lot in a Cutty. Thinking nothing of it, Bri told Action where we'd be that night. However, Action knew nothing about the sting operation involving Ink and Serve. Action had simply asked Rock to keep an eye on Bri and Mula. He was beginning to feel like a chump, being that Bri hadn't given him any pussy.

Yet, he was spending all his money on her. He wanted to see what nigga she was fucking with. Everybody was becoming a suspect in his mind. He wondered why Bri hung around so much, if she didn't wanna fuck?

***

"Yo, Rock, am I tripping? Or did it look like one of them thick pretty bitches had a gun?" G-Dep asked.

"Nigga gimme my damn weed!" Rock said, snatching the joint. "Hell yeah, you trippin'. Them hoes ain't have no damn gun. They were walking so damn close together, you wouldn't have seen one if they did." He laughed. "You need to leave this shit alone if you can't handle it." Rock took a pull of the Mary J blowing it in G-Dep's face. "Now, go in there and tell them two goofy ass niggas I said bring they asses out here and let's go! They let the hoes get away within forty-five minutes. They better have something good to tell me."

When G-Dep walked in the club, the twins recognized him right away as one of Action's and Rock's henchmen. When he scanned the crowd and walked directly over to Ink and Serve, they knew something sneaky was underway.

"Doe, you see this shit?" Moo asked, biting down on his toothpick.

"Yeah, I see it," Doe replied.

K'ajji

"Well, you know what time it is right?" He looked at his brother.

"Time to put these niggas on the fast track to hell," Doe replied.

"Murda-Murda!" Moo whispered with a smile.

"Um-hmm, they're leaving now. Stalk and kill. Let's get these niggas."

CHAPTER 44
DEATH AROUND THE CORNER

Dep, Serve and Ink exited the club talking shit to each other about all the pussy inside. When they got in the car with Rock, he instantly went in, grilling his cousin from the Chi on what they'd seen in the club. He turned to 'em in the back seat.

"What's up, niggas? What happened in there? Y'all see them bitches interacting wit' any niggas, or what?" He mugged them. "I see they were only in there for a minute."

Ink said, "I peeped 'em when they came in. Some nigga grabbed the tall thick one and walked her into VIP. The rest of 'em went to the bar, Joe."

"Yeah, them lil bitches got straight at us! Know what I'm saying?" Serve threw his two cents in, rubbing his hands together like he'd said something slick. He just knew he was on some player shit.

"What the fuck you talking 'bout?" Rock asked Ink.

Serve noticed an individual coming toward the car. "Shit, that look like the nigga she was talking to coming this way now!"

When Rock turned around in his seat to see who Serve was talking about, Doe was already at the window. Doe wore a smile on his face. Holding a .357 behind his right leg, he carefully watched the movement of the occupants inside. He had the gun cocked and ready.

Rock rolled down his window. He knew exactly who Doe was. He fucked with the dealer, slash killa on a few occasions. Trying to look past Doe, Rock was in search of Moo. The two were inseparable. You rarely saw one without the other. Since he didn't see 'em, he knew something was wrong. Still, he greeted Doe with enthusiasm.

"Doe!" Rock said, with a smile. It would be the hottest words he'd ever spoke.

Doe raised his gun and put it to his cheek. "Yeah, Doe, nigga!" *Booom!* He pulled the trigger.

G-Dep was hit in his face with a mixture of blood, teeth and saliva. It had gotten in his eyes, blinding him temporarily.

Shocked, Serve and Ink both panicked, yelling, "Oh shit! Oh shiit!" Moo rose from a crouching position on the other side of the car. He blew a hole in the passenger side window, blowing Dep's brains all over the windshield dashboard and Rock's lap. Doe released rounds at Serve and Ink in the back seat, as Ink fumbled with his cannon in an attempt to return fire. Moo gave Ink two to the chest, rocking him to sleep. Serve was shot in his neck and chest, but still gasping for air.

Doe sent his last slug through his forehead. Patrons in the parking lot ducked under cars, trying to stay alive as shots rang out. Moo and Doe could be heard laughing, as they fled the scene on foot. Back at their black Monte' Carlo, they jumped in and sped off into the night.

CHAPTER 45
IT'S JUST US AND THE GUNZ

When Action heard about Dep and Rock, he was Furious. It was six-thirty in the morning when his connect called him and told him to turn on the news. Reports indicated three men were executed in the parking lot of Red Corvette, and a fourth shot in the face was in critical condition. When the reporter said Rock and Dep's name his heart dropped. The other two names she'd mentioned didn't ring a bell. As always the police had no suspects. Action jumped out of bed and started getting dressed.

Zoi was awakened by all the sudden movement. "Baby, come back to bed. Where are you goin' this early?" She was still half asleep. Since he was one to never tell her everything, she wasn't expecting a full explanation.

"I gotta go handle something real quick. Something happened to Rock. I gotta go see what's up. Go back to sleep. I'll be back soon with some breakfast." He slapped her on her ass.

"Okay, babe." She rolled back over and closed her eyes.

Action went into the bathroom to handle his hygiene, then headed downstairs to call Dookie. He didn't want Zoi all in his business. He waltzed down the steps passing the living room, into the kitchen. He grabbed the phone off the wall and dialed Dookie's number but got no answer. After the tenth ring, he hung up and dialed it again. It was their code. This time he'd gotten an answer on the first ring.

"Hello! Dook!"

"Yeah," Dookie answered, sounding like he was still half asleep.

Dook, get yo' ass up, nigga! Rock and Dep got shot!"

"Wh-what? Stop playin' A, you serious? That's cuz."

Yeah, I'm serious. Dep dead and Rock in critical. I need you to go get some niggas together with some heat and meet me at the hospital!"

"Where they at?"

Which one? Damn, I don't even know. Most likely Froedert. I'm gon' call and make sure, then call you right back a'ight!"

"Hold up, dog! Who the fuck did this shit?"

"I don't know who did it. I'll call you right back!"

Action hung up and looked in the drawer next to it in search of the phone book. It wasn't there. He'd searched the cabinets over the frig and every drawer in the kitchen, nothing.

Then, he thought, *Maybe Zoi hasn't unpacked it yet. Let me check the boxes in the living room closet. I'm betting it's there.*

When he stepped into the living room he instantly froze. "What the fuck?"

Six figures sat in the dark on the living room's sofa. Hood reached for the lamp next to her and switched it on. Again, Action met six Gremlins guns at hand. Though he and Zoi had moved, their new location wasn't much of a secret due to her mouth.

"Don't worry about cha man Rock. He ain't gon' make it—I promise," Hood said in a manly voice. "But y'all might see each other again on the other side. Um-mm-mmm. Damn, you're kinda cute too." She shook her head at the fact he had to die.

"What y'all some kind of homosexual ass stickup kids or some shit!" He put his hands in the air, regretting he'd left his heat upstairs. Hood took off her mask. "*You!* You punk ass bitches!" He was in disbelief.

"Shhhh!" Hood shushed him, putting one in the chamber of one of her .45s then allowing it to rest gently against her lips. "Think," she mumbled against the gun. She tapped her temple with the other. "Whoever opens their eyes has to die. It's different this time. Now, you wouldn't want your wife and that son of yours to meet your same fate, would you?" She said. "Sweets, go to the top of the stairs. If anything moves, kill it."

Action shook his head, as sweat began to form on his brow.

Hood said, "Good thing my brothers saw ya man G-Dep hollerin' at them two dead ass niggas you sent to the club." She waved a .45 at him like a finger. "Shame, shame, shame."

"What?" he replied in a whispered tone.

The Streets Will Never Close 3

"This nigga trying to act dumb, y'all," Hood said. "I tell you what— You wanted to fuck Bri, right? Right, hot dick ass nigga? See where it got you? Bri, throw this nigga one of those big soft ass pillows so he can lay down. I'm gon' let Bri fuck you," she told him, like she was really about to do him a favor.

Bri took off her mask so he could see her. "You know, Action?" She tucked one of her Tre-8s at the small of her back. She grabbed a pillow from behind her. "I won a chess tournament when I was in eighth grade. I learned sacrifices have to be made all in the name of the king. My, how the game has now changed. See, today in your case—" She smiled. "The king must die to protect his queen and his prince. I guess we'll refer to him as your rook. Catch!" She tossed him the pillow.

Bri said, "Lay down for me," in a low sexy voice, she batted her eyes.

He sighed, but had no choice but to obey her in order to save his family. Dropping the pillow, he laid down placing his head on top of it.

"Umm-mmmm!" Sweets cocked her Shotty and went and stood over him pointing it at his head.

Bri said, "Nall, baby, cover your head with the pillow. It's gonna be okay," she told him with a look of assurance in her eyes.

She straddled his body, as if she were about to give him some. His eyes wandered in every direction. He was mumbling something under his breath as he inched the pillow from under his head, trying to find the courage to cover his face.

"Shhhhhh!" Bri hushed him, as she laid atop of him slowly guiding the pillow over his face.

Allowing her to do so, she jostled the pillow tightly against his face, put her .38 to it and pulled the trigger. The muffled blast sent feathers sprawling through the air.

"Throw me another one," she whispered.

She quickly replaced the first with the second, sending another round through Action's skull feathers were still dancing in the air as we made our exit.

165

CHAPTER 46
CONFUSED IN LOVE
Money

"You may have heard about all the suspicion surrounding Rock's death, since it gained national attention. It was all over the news. He wasn't a diabetic, but weeks after being shot. A mysterious woman dressed in a wig and a nurse's uniform walked into his hospital room and administered a huge dose of insulin as he laid comatose due to his injuries," Cyn said.

She used the spatula to place portions of her fluffy hot cheesy scrambled eggs on our plates. She'd made pancakes and bacon too. I was so hungry, I dug right in. I didn't even wait for her to sit down. She finished making her plate and joined me at the table. I was smacking my lips and licking my fingers as she sat down.

I said, "Damn, y'all fucked them niggas up." Then I took a gulp of my milk. As I continued to devour my breakfast. What she said next hit me like a ton of bricks. But now it all made sense.

She said, "Money, I have to be honest with you. I said all that to say this. . . Remember the night Hood introduced us?"

"Of course. How could I forget?"

She hung her head. Taking a deep breath, she then lifted her eyes toward the ceiling. Again, I saw the tears. She wasn't looking too good.

"Just tell 'em, Cyn," she spoke in third person.

"Wh-what's wrong. Tell me what?" I asked.

"You and Honor were supposed to be our next lick. There, I said it."

"Bitch, what! What you just say to me!" I slugged the plate of food and flipped the table separating us.

The dishes and the wood crashing to the floor was ear piercing. She didn't even flinch. She had no good reason to. As I noticed the mini Mac-10 that lay across her lap, seeing the gun pissed me off even more.

"What the fuck is that!"

"Papi, please calm down. I know you're angry with me. I wouldn't have told you shit if I didn't love you. You're my first and my only love. I have this because I didn't know how you'd react. I'm going to put it away now. We're family now. Taking from you would be taking from myself, taking from my daughter." She grabbed the Mac, stood up in her silky pink robe and made her way to the kitchen counter.

She had her back to me, opening the drawer, she placed it inside. She stared at it for a few seconds before slamming the drawer shut.

"I don't believe you'll hurt me. I-I—I'm sorry. I hope you understand. It wasn't personal. I didn't know you back then."

I was still sitting in my chair trying to think, fuming. I was madder than a muthafucka. I couldn't believe it. I was mad at her, but more disappointed in myself for slippin' so hard, so fast. I'd fallen in love with a woman that I'd barely known.

You could be dead right now! I thought.

Unable to think straight. Who was the woman? She'd been raped. She'd more than likely committed murder. Shit, even with all her crazy skeletons, I still love her. I had to get up outta there before I did something I'd regret. I went and grabbed the bricks out of the closet and headed toward the bedroom.

I heard her yelling, "Money, we need to talk!"

I wondered if Kilo was aware of the double life his sister led, and if he'd known I was once a target. Since so much money was being made, I also wondered why she'd indulge in some shit like that? I guess it was simply their hustle. Never in my right mind, would I have thought we were targets. Thinking with my dick, my stupid ass almost got hoodwinked.

When I came out of the room, she was sitting on the couch, rolling up some weed. Bags in hand, I paused and just looked at her.

She said, "Money, you forgive me?"

"Look, Cyn, I ain't got shit to say to you right now."

"Well, at least I told you. You ain't have to wake up to no bullshit phone call like I did. You could have told me that you had another woman. Wait, what did she say the other day? Wifey! You couldn't tell me that, huh?"

Knowing she was right, I ain't say shit. My mind was telling me I had to respect their gangsta. I'd laid up and laughed as she'd described how they banged out on niggas. It still hadn't dawned on me that I was prey to a bunch of predators. I got the rest of my shit. On the ride back to Racine, I thought about telling Honor and what he'd say. He'd most likely wanna get on some murder shit knowing him. Can't have that. This shit is far too embarrassing to bring to the squad period.

Before I left, Cyn told me I had sixty days to decide where I wanted to be. What do you think? I'm in love with two women, and I don't know what the fuck to do.

K'ajji

CHAPTER 47
Gina

It's three o'clock in the morning, and here I am on my way to investigate another homicide. This city is being dragged to shit. Things have to change and fast. We seem to be our own worst enemy. At this rate, the predictions made by the Census Bureau, Department of justice, and UW-Madison will become tragically true. Milwaukee will indeed become the murder capital in the near future.

Pulling to the curb in front of the brown duplex with jalousie windows, the yard was already taped off. Witnessing the scene, I unfettered a sigh. Patrol cars line the block like tanks, making our arrival seem more like an incursion than anything else. Amongst all the black faces of the neighborhood and the dangerous mixture of fear, anger and curiosity I spotted Jamison's blue Chevy parked at the apron of the driveway.

As always, I have to prepare myself for what I'm about to experience before I get out. Sending a silent prayer up to Yahweh, I ask for strength. My wandering mind was already trying to process how I'd have to break the news to yet another loving family. It's a problem because there's no easy way. Seeing that pain always seemed to blow my heart away. Though it's part of the job, it's something I refuse to grow used to.

If I allow my heart to harden or grow cold this shit will become normal to me and it's not! I hopped out of the Vic ready to get to it. Jamison walked toward me in his tan trench as I climbed the concrete steps leading to the porch landing. I noticed that his eyebrows are fused in a straight line. His face is saddened, which tells me it has to be something gruesome. He has thick skin. It takes a lot to get this type of reaction out of him.

"Aw, shit, J—" I pulled on the gloves I'd retrieved from my pocket. "You're scaring me. What we got?"

He heaved a sigh. "A bit of an overkill inside. Females, African American. My guess, twenty to twenty-five years old. The friend here called. Says she found her." He pointed in the direction of his car.

I turned, to see a young lady wrapped in a red blanket seated in the rear of the vehicle. She was being questioned by Officer Handon.

"She's been living here for about two years."

"Canvass?"

"So far, nobody has said a thing besides the old lady next door that has sheets for curtains. Says she saw three people speed off in a black Cadillac moments after she heard what she thought were screams."

"Whose apartment is this, the friend or the victim?"

"The friend. Apparently, the deceased was the best friend and babysitter. We found a toddler in the attic. He'd been up there for quite some time."

"How old?"

"Three. Name Nomi—he's with Protective Services for the time being. Had to have him checked out. I mean, just to be on the safe side. You know?"

"Riiight-right." I nodded.

"A few more things, then I'll let you go. The kid says his Tee-Tee, one of whom I assume is the deceased, told him to hide and not to come out until she or his mother came for him. What he heard had to horrify him. He sure as hell wouldn't come out for us. The mother called his name for at least ten minutes," he spoke with his hands.

"Smart kid. I wanna talk to him. Is that all? I'm ready for my walk through."

"Yeah, that's it. Have your way," he replied.

"Where is she?"

"It's a two bed, one bath. You'll find her in the bathroom. He walked down the steps toward his car.

"And where you goin'?" I asked.

"To try and get us some more answers!" he yelled over his shoulder.

"Did you—"

"Nope, I didn't touch anything."

There were no signs of forced entry, which was my first mental note. Walking into the residence there was that same retired silence that always seems to loom over me before encountering the dead. All was in order in the hallway. Nothing unusual. Side by side pictures on the walls. I'm assuming they're of the young lady that lives here and her son. There's a guy in one of the photos that wasn't mentioned as being a resident. Is he on the lease? The child's father? The husband or boyfriend? Something to look into.

Me, knowing the inevitable, my heart sped up. There I was wishing I was at home curled up with a spoon and my half-gallon of Haagen-Daz ice cream. Entering the living room, I could see that whoever she was, she'd fought for her life. The orderliness was now gone. The apartment was in shambles, blood spatter on the eggshell white walls, the overturned furniture, along with the trail of blood on the hardwood floor told a story of its own.

The television was still on. She'd been watching BET. The coffee table that sat in front of the tan upholstered sofa was smashed. One of the two lamps that sat on each side of the couch had been slung across the room. The window curtains were open. No blinds meant she'd seen her attacker pull up. Being she'd told the child to hide, I'm sure she knew this visit wouldn't be a friendly one. When someone is murdered, nine times out of ten it's by someone they knew.

Now, I'd have to connect the dots. I'd have to find out who she'd associated with. If she had a dude in her life, and who'd want her dead as I searched for who the killer or killers might be. In the small kitchen the cabinets and the drawers hung open as if someone was in search of something. I noticed a butcher knife was missing from the set's holder on the countertop. Possibly the murder weapon?

Checking the bedrooms of the mother and her little boy, I found that they too had been searched. I found mail addressed to a Ms. Waters in her room all over the floor. The name rang a bell. Where did I know it from? When all was said and done, I ended up in the bathroom. It was a bloody mess from the floor to the ceiling. Everything went black and white inside me as the sound of dripping water in the bathroom's sink pinged inside the drain. It seemed to echo.

I began to feel like I was on the set of a classic Alfred Hitchcock Movie. The shower curtain was pulled closed. Toiletries, soap, shampoo, the toothpaste, toothbrushes, razors., combs, curling irons, makeup kit and towels were all cast about and covered in blood. Physically, my victim's leg was the only thing visible to me as it hung over the edge of the tub. I had to actually go back to my car and grab some booties to cover my feet before entering the bathroom. When I returned, I went in and pulled the curtain back.

Her body was twisted. She was wearing a pair of white GUESS jeans with a green, white and gold T-Shirt bearing the words, *Mrs. Chocolate*. Her left sock was still on her foot. I'd found its match in the kitchen. She'd kicked and fought as long as she could. Laying on her right side, she faced away from me.

She'd been stabbed to death. Counting her wounds. She'd been stabbed some sixty-two times or more. She had defensive wounds in her hands. She had seven-hundred-dollar bills, but no identification. Reaching for her chin, I slowly moved her head so I could see her face.

My God! It's Fatima.

Though our time together was brief. It hurt my soul to see someone had done this to this girl. It damn near brought me to tears.

I noticed her right hand was clenched. She seemed to have something inside. When I opened her hand, I saw something else that made me gasp. It was a cross. One identical to the one I wear around my neck. Was God really seeing all this? I grabbed it, and quickly placed it in my pocket. I went back in time, thinking of that special moment the gold necklaces were handed to me and my sister.

They'd been given to us by our mother before she passed. Handmade, they're unique. The mold was broken. There aren't any crucifixes like mine, hers' and my mothers. I knew if she hadn't done it, she was certainly here. I had to protect her if I could. I thought about a poem I once read by Langston Hughes. He wrote about death and how it never announced itself. It didn't care what you had to do. It simply came and stole you like a thief in the night. That's how it came and got my mom. Sometimes I wonder am I a fool for pain, for always trying to catch him. Flying toward death like a moth to a flame. I doubled back to make sure I hadn't missed anything that could place my sister at the scene. Now I had to find out what the friend knew.

Back on the porch, I called the Crime Scene techs in. They needed to do their fingerprint analysis before rigor mortis set in.

"So, what do you think?" Jamison asked.

"I don't know," I replied. "The canvass?"

"Nothing," he shrugged. Her friend was still seated in the back of the squad. She seemed a little too calm for me.

"Where you going?" he questioned, as I walked over to her.

"I need a witness, Jamison. I need to talk to this girl. Find me a witness!" I didn't bother looking back.

I was hoping like hell the devil was a lie, and my sis had not done this. But shit wasn't looking good. I opened the back door of the squad and peered inside.

"I know you!" I told the young lady I hadn't recognized her, because she looked different from her mugshot. I was looking at a potential problem. Beautiful, she had a resemblance to Erika Ash. However, one look at her in person, I could tell she was a prissy little bitch.

"I don't think so," she replied.

"You're right." I nodded. "I know of you. Your name is Alexus Waters. I read your sheet a few months ago."

"Yeah? So, what. And?"

"And! That girl had a million-and-one reasons not to come back! Now she's dead! I wanna know what the hell she was doing here. And yo' ass gon' tell me!"

To Be Continued…
The Streets Will Never Close 4

K'ajji

Coming Soon

Lock Down Publications and Ca$h Presents assisted publishing packages.

BASIC PACKAGE $499
Editing
Cover Design
Formatting

UPGRADED PACKAGE $800
Typing
Editing
Cover Design
Formatting

ADVANCE PACKAGE $1,200
Typing
Editing
Cover Design
Formatting
Copyright registration
Proofreading
Upload book to Amazon

LDP SUPREME PACKAGE $1,500
Typing
Editing
Cover Design
Formatting
Copyright registration
Proofreading
Set up Amazon account
Upload book to Amazon
Advertise on LDP Amazon and Facebook page

K'ajji

***Other services available upon request. Additional charges may apply
Lock Down Publications
P.O. Box 944
Stockbridge, GA 30281-9998
Phone # 470 303-9761

Submission Guideline

Submit the first three chapters of your completed manuscript to ldpsubmissions@gmail.com, subject line: Your book's title. The manuscript must be in a .doc file and sent as an attachment. Document should be in Times New Roman, double spaced and in size 12 font. Also, provide your synopsis and full contact information. If sending multiple submissions, they must each be in a separate email.

Have a story but no way to send it electronically? You can still submit to LDP/Ca$h Presents. Send in the first three chapters, written or typed, of your completed manuscript to:

**LDP: Submissions Dept
Po Box 944
Stockbridge, Ga 30281**

DO NOT send original manuscript. Must be a duplicate.

Provide your synopsis and a cover letter containing your full contact information.

Thanks for considering LDP and Ca$h Presents.

NEW RELEASES

THE COCAINE PRINCESS 3 by KING RIO
THE BILLIONAIRE BENTLEYS 3 by VON DIESEL
COKE GIRLZ by ROMELL TUKES
VICIOIUS LOYALTY 2 by KINGPEN
THE STREETS WILL NEVER CLOSE 3 by K'AJJI

The Streets Will Never Close 3

Coming Soon from Lock Down Publications/Ca$h Presents
BLOOD OF A BOSS VI
SHADOWS OF THE GAME II
TRAP BASTARD II
By **Askari**
LOYAL TO THE GAME IV
By **T.J. & Jelissa**
IF TRUE SAVAGE VIII
MIDNIGHT CARTEL IV
DOPE BOY MAGIC IV
CITY OF KINGZ III
NIGHTMARE ON SILENT AVE II
THE PLUG OF LIL MEXICO II
By **Chris Green**
BLAST FOR ME III
A SAVAGE DOPEBOY III
CUTTHROAT MAFIA III
DUFFLE BAG CARTEL VII
HEARTLESS GOON VI
By **Ghost**
A HUSTLER'S DECEIT III
KILL ZONE II
BAE BELONGS TO ME III
By **Aryanna**
KING OF THE TRAP III
By **T.J. Edwards**
GORILLAZ IN THE BAY V
3X KRAZY III
STRAIGHT BEAST MODE II
De'Kari

K'ajji

KINGPIN KILLAZ IV
STREET KINGS III
PAID IN BLOOD III
CARTEL KILLAZ IV
DOPE GODS III
Hood Rich
SINS OF A HUSTLA II
ASAD
RICH $AVAGE II
By Martell Troublesome Bolden
YAYO V
Bred In The Game 2
S. Allen
CREAM III
THE STREETS WILL TALK II
By Yolanda Moore
SON OF A DOPE FIEND III
HEAVEN GOT A GHETTO II
By Renta
LOYALTY AIN'T PROMISED III
By Keith Williams
I'M NOTHING WITHOUT HIS LOVE II
SINS OF A THUG II
TO THE THUG I LOVED BEFORE II
IN A HUSTLER I TRUST II
By Monet Dragun
QUIET MONEY IV
EXTENDED CLIP III
THUG LIFE IV
By **Trai'Quan**

The Streets Will Never Close 3

THE STREETS MADE ME IV
By **Larry D. Wright**
IF YOU CROSS ME ONCE II
By **Anthony Fields**
THE STREETS WILL NEVER CLOSE IV
By **K'ajji**
HARD AND RUTHLESS III
KILLA KOUNTY III
By **Khufu**
MONEY GAME III
By **Smoove Dolla**
JACK BOYS VS DOPE BOYS II
A GANGSTA'S QUR'AN V
COKE GIRLZ II
By **Romell Tukes**
MURDA WAS THE CASE II
Elijah R. Freeman
THE STREETS NEVER LET GO II
By **Robert Baptiste**
AN UNFORESEEN LOVE III
By **Meesha**
KING OF THE TRENCHES III
by **GHOST & TRANAY ADAMS**
MONEY MAFIA II
LOYAL TO THE SOIL III
By **Jibril Williams**
QUEEN OF THE ZOO II
By **Black Migo**
THE BRICK MAN IV
THE COCAINE PRINCESS IV

K'ajji

By King Rio
VICIOUS LOYALTY III
By Kingpen
A GANGSTA'S PAIN II
By J-Blunt
CONFESSIONS OF A JACKBOY III
By Nicholas Lock
GRIMEY WAYS II
By Ray Vinci
KING KILLA II
By Vincent "Vitto" Holloway
BETRAYAL OF A THUG II
By Fre$h

Available Now

RESTRAINING ORDER **I & II**
By **CA$H & Coffee**
LOVE KNOWS NO BOUNDARIES **I II & III**
By **Coffee**
RAISED AS A GOON I, II, III & IV
BRED BY THE SLUMS I, II, III
BLAST FOR ME I & II
ROTTEN TO THE CORE I II III

The Streets Will Never Close 3

A BRONX TALE I, II, III
DUFFLE BAG CARTEL I II III IV V VI
HEARTLESS GOON I II III IV V
A SAVAGE DOPEBOY I II
DRUG LORDS I II III
CUTTHROAT MAFIA I II
KING OF THE TRENCHES
By **Ghost**
LAY IT DOWN **I & II**
LAST OF A DYING BREED I II
BLOOD STAINS OF A SHOTTA I & II III
By **Jamaica**
LOYAL TO THE GAME I II III
LIFE OF SIN I, II III
By **TJ & Jelissa**
BLOODY COMMAS I & II
SKI MASK CARTEL I II & III
KING OF NEW YORK I II,III IV V
RISE TO POWER I II III
COKE KINGS I II III IV V
BORN HEARTLESS I II III IV
KING OF THE TRAP I II
By **T.J. Edwards**
IF LOVING HIM IS WRONG…I & II
LOVE ME EVEN WHEN IT HURTS I II III
By **Jelissa**
WHEN THE STREETS CLAP BACK I & II III
THE HEART OF A SAVAGE I II III
MONEY MAFIA
LOYAL TO THE SOIL I II

K'ajji

By **Jibril Williams**
A DISTINGUISHED THUG STOLE MY HEART I II & III
LOVE SHOULDN'T HURT I II III IV
RENEGADE BOYS I II III IV
PAID IN KARMA I II III
SAVAGE STORMS I II III
AN UNFORESEEN LOVE I II

By **Meesha**
A GANGSTER'S CODE I &, II III
A GANGSTER'S SYN I II III
THE SAVAGE LIFE I II III
CHAINED TO THE STREETS I II III
BLOOD ON THE MONEY I II III
A GANGSTA'S PAIN

By **J-Blunt**
PUSH IT TO THE LIMIT

By **Bre' Hayes**
BLOOD OF A BOSS **I, II, III, IV, V**
SHADOWS OF THE GAME
TRAP BASTARD

By **Askari**
THE STREETS BLEED MURDER **I, II & III**
THE HEART OF A GANGSTA I II& III

By **Jerry Jackson**
CUM FOR ME I II III IV V VI VII VIII

An **LDP Erotica Collaboration**
BRIDE OF A HUSTLA **I II & II**
THE FETTI GIRLS **I, II& III**
CORRUPTED BY A GANGSTA I, II III, IV
BLINDED BY HIS LOVE

The Streets Will Never Close 3

THE PRICE YOU PAY FOR LOVE I, II ,III
DOPE GIRL MAGIC I II III
By **Destiny Skai**
WHEN A GOOD GIRL GOES BAD
By **Adrienne**
THE COST OF LOYALTY I II III
By **Kweli**
A GANGSTER'S REVENGE **I II III & IV**
THE BOSS MAN'S DAUGHTERS I II III IV V
A SAVAGE LOVE **I & II**
BAE BELONGS TO ME I II
A HUSTLER'S DECEIT I, II, III
WHAT BAD BITCHES DO I, II, III
SOUL OF A MONSTER I II III
KILL ZONE
A DOPE BOY'S QUEEN I II III
By **Aryanna**
A KINGPIN'S AMBITON
A KINGPIN'S AMBITION **II**
I MURDER FOR THE DOUGH
By **Ambitious**
TRUE SAVAGE I II III IV V VI VII
DOPE BOY MAGIC I, II, III
MIDNIGHT CARTEL I II III
CITY OF KINGZ I II
NIGHTMARE ON SILENT AVE
THE PLUG OF LIL MEXICO II

By **Chris Green**
A DOPEBOY'S PRAYER

K'ajji

By **Eddie "Wolf" Lee**
THE KING CARTEL **I, II & III**
By **Frank Gresham**
THESE NIGGAS AIN'T LOYAL **I, II & III**
By **Nikki Tee**
GANGSTA SHYT **I II &III**
By **CATO**
THE ULTIMATE BETRAYAL
By **Phoenix**
BOSS'N UP **I , II & III**
By **Royal Nicole**
I LOVE YOU TO DEATH
By **Destiny J**
I RIDE FOR MY HITTA
I STILL RIDE FOR MY HITTA
By **Misty Holt**
LOVE & CHASIN' PAPER
By **Qay Crockett**
TO DIE IN VAIN
SINS OF A HUSTLA
By **ASAD**
BROOKLYN HUSTLAZ
By **Boogsy Morina**
BROOKLYN ON LOCK I & II
By **Sonovia**
GANGSTA CITY
By **Teddy Duke**
A DRUG KING AND HIS DIAMOND I & II III
A DOPEMAN'S RICHES
HER MAN, MINE'S TOO I, II

The Streets Will Never Close 3

CASH MONEY HO'S
THE WIFEY I USED TO BE I II
By Nicole Goosby
TRAPHOUSE KING **I II & III**
KINGPIN KILLAZ I II III
STREET KINGS I II
PAID IN BLOOD **I II**
CARTEL KILLAZ I II III
DOPE GODS I II
By **Hood Rich**
LIPSTICK KILLAH **I, II, III**
CRIME OF PASSION I II & III
FRIEND OR FOE I II III
By **Mimi**
STEADY MOBBN' **I, II, III**
THE STREETS STAINED MY SOUL I II III
By **Marcellus Allen**
WHO SHOT YA **I, II, III**
SON OF A DOPE FIEND I II
HEAVEN GOT A GHETTO
Renta
GORILLAZ IN THE BAY **I II III IV**
TEARS OF A GANGSTA I II
3X KRAZY I II
STRAIGHT BEAST MODE
DE'KARI
TRIGGADALE I II III
MURDAROBER WAS THE CASE
Elijah R. Freeman
GOD BLESS THE TRAPPERS I, II, III

K'ajji

THESE SCANDALOUS STREETS I, II, III
FEAR MY GANGSTA I, II, III IV, V
THESE STREETS DON'T LOVE NOBODY I, II
BURY ME A G I, II, III, IV, V
A GANGSTA'S EMPIRE I, II, III, IV
THE DOPEMAN'S BODYGAURD I II
THE REALEST KILLAZ I II III
THE LAST OF THE OGS I II III
Tranay Adams
THE STREETS ARE CALLING
Duquie Wilson
MARRIED TO A BOSS I II III
By Destiny Skai & Chris Green
KINGZ OF THE GAME I II III IV V VI
Playa Ray
SLAUGHTER GANG I II III
RUTHLESS HEART I II III
By Willie Slaughter
FUK SHYT
By Blakk Diamond
DON'T F#CK WITH MY HEART I II
By Linnea
ADDICTED TO THE DRAMA I II III
IN THE ARM OF HIS BOSS II
By Jamila
YAYO I II III IV
A SHOOTER'S AMBITION I II
BRED IN THE GAME
By S. Allen
TRAP GOD I II III

The Streets Will Never Close 3

RICH $AVAGE
MONEY IN THE GRAVE I II III
By Martell Troublesome Bolden
FOREVER GANGSTA
GLOCKS ON SATIN SHEETS I II
By Adrian Dulan
TOE TAGZ I II III IV
LEVELS TO THIS SHYT I II
By Ah'Million
KINGPIN DREAMS I II III
By Paper Boi Rari
CONFESSIONS OF A GANGSTA I II III IV
CONFESSIONS OF A JACKBOY I II
By Nicholas Lock
I'M NOTHING WITHOUT HIS LOVE
SINS OF A THUG
TO THE THUG I LOVED BEFORE
A GANGSTA SAVED XMAS
IN A HUSTLER I TRUST
By Monet Dragun
CAUGHT UP IN THE LIFE I II III
THE STREETS NEVER LET GO
By Robert Baptiste
NEW TO THE GAME I II III
MONEY, MURDER & MEMORIES I II III
By **Malik D. Rice**
LIFE OF A SAVAGE I II III
A GANGSTA'S QUR'AN I II III IV
MURDA SEASON I II III
GANGLAND CARTEL I II III

K'ajji

CHI'RAQ GANGSTAS I II III
KILLERS ON ELM STREET I II III
JACK BOYZ N DA BRONX I II III
A DOPEBOY'S DREAM I II III
JACK BOYS VS DOPE BOYS
COKE GIRLZ
By Romell Tukes
LOYALTY AIN'T PROMISED I II
By Keith Williams
QUIET MONEY I II III
THUG LIFE I II III
EXTENDED CLIP I II
By **Trai'Quan**
THE STREETS MADE ME I II III
By **Larry D. Wright**
THE ULTIMATE SACRIFICE I, II, III, IV, V, VI
KHADIFI
IF YOU CROSS ME ONCE
ANGEL I II
IN THE BLINK OF AN EYE
By **Anthony Fields**
THE LIFE OF A HOOD STAR
By Ca$h & Rashia Wilson
THE STREETS WILL NEVER CLOSE I II III
By K'ajji
CREAM I II
THE STREETS WILL TALK
By Yolanda Moore
NIGHTMARES OF A HUSTLA I II III
By King Dream

The Streets Will Never Close 3

CONCRETE KILLA I II
VICIOUS LOYALTY I II
By Kingpen
HARD AND RUTHLESS I II
MOB TOWN 251
THE BILLIONAIRE BENTLEYS I II III
By Von Diesel
GHOST MOB
Stilloan Robinson
MOB TIES I II III IV V
By SayNoMore
BODYMORE MURDERLAND I II III
By Delmont Player
FOR THE LOVE OF A BOSS
By C. D. Blue
MOBBED UP I II III IV
THE BRICK MAN I II III
THE COCAINE PRINCESS I II
By King Rio
KILLA KOUNTY I II III
By Khufu
MONEY GAME I II
By Smoove Dolla
A GANGSTA'S KARMA I II
By FLAME
KING OF THE TRENCHES I II
by **GHOST & TRANAY ADAMS**
QUEEN OF THE ZOO
By **Black Migo**
GRIMEY WAYS

K'ajji

By Ray Vinci
XMAS WITH AN ATL SHOOTER
By Ca$h & Destiny Skai
KING KILLA
By Vincent "Vitto" Holloway
BETRAYAL OF A THUG
By Fre$h

The Streets Will Never Close 3

BOOKS BY LDP'S CEO, CA$H

TRUST IN NO MAN
TRUST IN NO MAN 2
TRUST IN NO MAN 3
BONDED BY BLOOD
SHORTY GOT A THUG
THUGS CRY
THUGS CRY 2
THUGS CRY 3
TRUST NO BITCH
TRUST NO BITCH 2
TRUST NO BITCH 3
TIL MY CASKET DROPS
RESTRAINING ORDER
RESTRAINING ORDER 2
IN LOVE WITH A CONVICT
LIFE OF A HOOD STAR
XMAS WITH AN ATL SHOOTER

K'ajji